THE SUMMER
OF MOONLIGHT
SECRETS

BOOKS BY DANETTE HAWORTH

Violet Raines Almost Got Struck by Lightning
The Summer of Moonlight Secrets
Me & Jack

The Summer of Moonlight Secrets

Danette Haworth

WALKER & COMPANY
New York

For my mom, Joan,

who inspires me in every way

First published in the United States of America in June 2010
by Walker Publishing Company, Inc., a division of Bloomsbury Publishing, Inc.
Paperback edition published in May 2011
www.bloomsburykids.com

For information about permission to reproduce selections from this book, write to
Permissions, Walker BFYR, 175 Fifth Avenue, New York, New York 10010

The Library of Congress has cataloged the hardcover edition as follows:
Haworth, Danette.
The summer of moonlight secrets / by Danette Haworth.
p.   cm.
Summary: During the summer of 1987, Allie Jo, whose family runs an antebellum Florida
hotel, meets Chase, who is staying there with his father, and they become friends when
they discover a mysterious teenager hiding on the grounds of the hotel.
ISBN-13: 978-0-8027-9520-5 • ISBN-10: 0-8027-9520-X (hardcover)
[1. Selkies—Fiction. 2. Hotels, motels, etc.—Fiction. 3. Families—Fiction.
4. Interpersonal relations—Fiction. 5. Florida—Fiction.] I. Title.
PZ7.H31365Su 2010   [Fic]—dc22   2009037053

ISBN: 978-0-8027-2291-1 (paperback)

Book design by Nicole Gastonguay
Typeset by Westchester Book Composition
Printed in the U.S.A. by Quad/Graphics, Fairfield, Pennsylvania
2 4 6 8 10 9 7 5 3 1

All papers used by Bloomsbury Publishing, Inc., are natural, recyclable products
made from wood grown in well-managed forests. The manufacturing processes
conform to the environmental regulations of the country of origin.

1

"Hey!" I yell.

I don't know who I'm yelling at; I can't see them. But I was lying out on the concrete pad around Hope Springs—Hope Springs Eternal, if you want the full name—with my face turned up to the sun, letting it press its golden rays on my face. Later today, the sun will fry the skin right off your bones.

So I was lying here all peaceful. Quiet. No tourists, which are the worst kind of trespassers. Until suddenly I hear a crash, someone jumping into the water on the other side. I sit up real straight, lean forward, and watch as a girl glides through the water, fast as a sailfish. Her hair flows behind her like a fin and she flashes with color. I sit even straighter now; why is she wearing regular clothes in the water?

Two hands grip the edge of the wall that surrounds the springhead, and she rises from the water.

"Hey!" I yell again, recoiling from the ice-cold splatters.

Water streams down her face, causing her to squeeze her eyes. She pushes her hair back and pops her eyes open. They are as black as midnight.

She smiles at me as she hoists herself out of the water, fully clothed in jean shorts and a black and purple T-shirt. "Hello to you," she says.

I gape at her.

She's so pretty. Her long, dark hair shimmers with blue, reflecting the sun and water. She leans her head to the side, grabs her hair into a twist, and squeezes the water out.

Pointing to the hotel, she asks, "Would that door be open?"

I nod dumbly.

She flashes her Colgate smile again and winks at me.

I turn and watch as she glides up the lawn to The Meriwether. She barely pauses as she passes the dock and snatches a towel right off a cabinet.

Just as she slips into the side door, my brain starts working again and I want to call out the rules to her: *No running. No diving. Towels must be checked out.*

She's broken every one of them.

And worse, the side door she just went in is Employees Only.

When I see her again, I'm going to have to set her straight. This used to be a five-star hotel; you can't be running around all splashing and grabbing things like that. But at the same time, she smiled as if she knew me. And when she winked, it was like she was including me in on a secret, just me and her.

Staring up at The Meriwether, I scan the hotel, but I see no movement, no sign of her in the windows. I look down at the concrete where she just passed. Already, her footprints are disappearing.

2

Chase

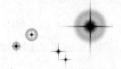

Twenty-two hours cooped up in the car is enough for me. My butt's sore and I'm bored out of my skull.

"What're we gonna do first?" I ask Dad. I grab the pamphlets and scan them: parasailing, surfing, skimboarding, waterskiing. Ah, man, I can't choose; they all sound good.

Dad cranks the wheel and we turn down a boulevard lined with palm trees. "I don't know about you, but I'm going to sleep."

"What?" Is he kidding me? I've been sitting in this car for a whole day, eating nothing but drive-through junk just so we could get here faster. Florida is a long way from Ohio.

"Yeah," Dad says. "I didn't get to take naps like you did."

"I didn't take any naps."

Dad smirks. "Yes, you did."

"No, I didn't. I may have rested my eyes, but I didn't sleep." Hey, it gets boring watching scenery pass by.

"Well, you rested your eyes for about three hours a while ago." He takes a sip from a Styrofoam coffee cup. Where did he get that? Maybe I *did* fall asleep.

I shrug my shoulders. "But you're not really going to sleep, are you? It's only"—I glance at the clock on the dash—"eight thirty in the morning."

"Oh, good." Yawning, he rubs the back of his neck, then cracks it sideways. "I can sleep all day."

"What's the point of driving all night if you're just going to sleep all day?"

"Chase," he says, turning to me. His face droops; okay, okay, he does look tired. But sleeping all day? I can't be stuck in a hotel room on top of this drive.

None of the pamphlets in my hands show a guy taking a nap. "What am I going to do while you're sleeping?"

He shrugs. "You can watch TV—quietly."

Yes! That's what I came to Florida for—quiet TV watching. "Dad! Come on!"

He takes a quick look at me and sighs. "How about we check in, get some decent breakfast, and see how we feel after that?"

I nod, knowing I'll talk him into something over breakfast.

We turn from the boulevard down a drive that cuts through rolling hills.

"I thought Florida was flat," I say.

"Not all of it," Dad says. "Besides, this is hotel property. In the old days, this used to be a golf course." Of course he would know that; he researched The Meriwether for the travel series he's writing.

He scans the horizon. I know what he's doing—he's writing. He's always writing. Even with no paper or pen, he takes notes constantly. I bet if I tapped into his brain I'd hear, *Century-old oaks shaded the lawn, their branches covered*—no—*their branches arrayed in the finery of Spanish moss.*

I've read enough of his stuff to write it for him. *You're a natural*, he's told me. *You write like someone much older than yourself.* It's true. It catches even me by surprise sometimes. I'll just be looking at something and my thoughts slip into a fancy way of speaking. My teachers all say I'm a good writer, too; they read my stories out loud.

I stare out the window. I thought this place would be all palm trees, but it's mainly oaks with heavy branches that dip low, some touching the ground before curving back up.

We climb a bridge and the hotel springs into view. It's like stepping into the old days. The place is like four or five stories tall, with peaked roofs and trim that Dad told me come from being built in the Victorian era. Mold eats at the wood under the windows, making the pale yellow paint look dirty. The porch colors are faded—purple, orange, and green—happy colors from a long time ago. Green shutters are missing from half the windows; a couple of them dangle at the sides.

Could a place like this even have cable?

We carry our suitcases in and stop at the front desk, where the guy is on the phone. College dude. Sandy hair, lanky build. He smiles at us and holds a finger up to Dad— *Just a minute!*

I put my skateboard down and push one foot on it. Nice! Great wood floor. "I'm going to look around," I say.

Dad's shoulders drop. "Just stay here." He glances at the guy, who is now flipping through paperwork, still on the phone.

I kick up my board and hold it. The hall stretches for miles. It's dark, lit up by chandeliers, and carpet covers the wood floor beyond the lobby. I see all kinds of alcoves and stairwells. "I'm going to check it out," I say, wandering away from Dad.

"Chase!" he says, but he's using the voice that means he's already given in. He knows he can't hold on to me.

This place is cool. The hallway is like a little street with tiny shops on both sides—an ice-cream store, a restaurant, a bakery. I'm not buying anything, though; I want to explore. I stop at a staircase that spirals up into darkness. Leaning against the handrail, I peer through the balusters.

"Dad!" I yell. He's still standing at the desk, waiting. I motion to the stairs. "I'm going up there!"

I can see his frown from here.

"I'll be right back!" The stairs are calling me. *Come on!*

He rolls his eyes. "You better be," he yells.

I'm taking the stairs two at a time when I hear him add, "And don't get in trouble!"

I just laugh.

3

Allie Jo

The best place to eat The Meriwether's Famous Blueberry Pancakes is in the crook of the bay window in the Emerald Dining Room. That's where Dad, Mom, and I are sitting, but I finish off that blueberry goodness in about two minutes and then I lick the maple syrup clean off the plate.

"Allie Jo," Dad says, setting his coffee down. "That plate is *spit-polished*. Just put it back in and give it to the next person." What a joker. He picks up his cup. "Time to get busy," he says, kissing the top of my head before walking on out of here to his office.

"No tours today," Mom says, "so I'll be helping Dad in the office." She gives me a quick squeeze before reaching out for Dad's hand. I watch them walk out of the dining room together. Lovebirds!

I myself am not quite ready to get started, so I lean back in my chair and scan the dining room. That girl from this morning isn't here. If she wants pancakes, she'd better hurry; Chef shuts breakfast down in fifteen minutes.

I pull my legs up and sit crisscross on the chair, staring out the window until the cooks come and break down the buffet. A red cardinal perches on the bird feeder by the oak. I watch as he pushes his head through the feeder, showering the grass with black sunflower seeds and a mix of little yellow seeds. His wife pecks through the grass. When a squirrel jumps from an oak branch onto the bird feeder, both cardinals keep eating. I guess they're used to him.

Well, that's enough sitting on my butt for one morning. Time to get started on my rounds.

Passing the mostly empty tables, I carry my dishes to the cart at the back of the dining room: silverware goes into the plastic cylinder; plates go on one side of the bus tub, glasses on the other. Guests don't bus their own tables, but since I live at The Meriwether, I have to clear my own dishes, even though they don't pay me.

"Hay, Clay," I say, passing the front desk. I laugh to myself because I know he thinks I said, "Hey, Clay." It's just one of those private jokes I have with myself.

He nods to me. "Allie Jo."

I get to the far staircase and dash up the stairs. As I climb past the second floor, I reach the sign that says, *The Meriwether is renovating the upper floors for your future enjoyment. For your personal safety, please enjoy the amenities on the lower floors.* And then, just in case you don't understand what that really means, square black letters at the bottom say, *Guests Prohibited.* I step over the velvet cord and continue.

Everything changes as I turn on the landing. The sculpted floral carpet ends; the stairs going up are covered by all kinds of different rugs, depending on when or if that story got renovated. Which some of them did, but that was a long time ago, not anytime soon, as that sign would have you believe. That's what makes these floors so interesting—you're walking on actual history.

The air gets warmer the higher I go. Even the smell changes—a hint of cut grass, a trace of mildew—but mainly it's the smell of heat and wood. It's a good smell.

I turn onto the third floor to begin my inspection. They don't pay me for this either, but, you know, someone's got to do it. This floor has no rug on account of the hotel being sold in the middle of the 1972 restoration. Just as I'm coming up on the Beauford Chambers Suite, I spot a boy down the hall.

"Hey!" I yell.

He whips his head around, sees me, and grins. Then he throws down a skateboard and pumps like a hundred miles an hour.

I tear after him. "Get back here!" I holler. That's antique heart of pine he's rolling that stupid board over.

4

Chase

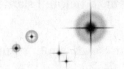

Guests Prohibited. Are you kidding me? I lift my skateboard and climb over the rope. Dad's checking us into this place, and I'm checking it out. It's like a creepy old mansion. The stairs groan under my feet. A deep crack spreads from one side of the staircase to the other, and the rug looks older and dirty.

When I reach the next level, the wood floor rolls out in front of me—the perfect surface. The sign said they're renovating this floor, but I don't see any workers. Still, I better be sure. I carry my skateboard and walk down the hall.

"Hey!"

I whip my head around and see a girl standing all sergeantlike, hands on her hips, legs apart. I grin, throw my board down, and I'm off.

"Get back here!" she bellows.

I laugh. "Come and get me!"

I'm flying over the whoop-de-doos, getting a little air, faster, faster! Yeah! I stamp my back foot down for a perfect ollie, only my landing's sketchy and I feel one of the wheels catch in a groove. Suddenly I'm cartwheeling—arms flailing, legs snapping—and I have just enough time to think, *This is gonna hurt!* before I slam onto the floor.

Aw, man.

I'm squeezing my eyes shut, trying to decide which hurts more—my head or my ego—when I hear that girl come running up.

"Are you okay?" she yells.

I lift my head, try to look at her, and suddenly feel like I'm gonna hurl. I rest my head. Closing my eyes, I say, "Yeah, I just need to lie down for a minute."

Her footsteps shuffle up close to me.

She gasps.

My eyes snap open. "What?"

Gaping, she points at my arm. "It's crooked," she says.

Oh, no. I try to sit up, but when I brace myself, fire races down my right arm. Oh, man. "I'm gonna be sick."

Her face goes white. Mine feels green. "I better get my dad," she says, and before I can say anything she takes off, leaving me alone on the floor.

Waves of seasickness overtake me. My arm throbs like

a blinking red light. I moan. Then, because no one's around, I moan louder.

It's on a freshwater spring, Dad had said. *You'll love it—lots of history.* Um, yeah, that's what I want on summer vacation—history. An old, beat-up hotel with bad floors. I know he's a travel writer and everything, but how come we never go where *I* want to go, like that place that had shrunken heads outside and the sign read, *Heading this way?*

What's taking so long? It hurts too much to just wait. If I had a mother, she'd already be here with an ice pack. I roll on my left side and part of my right arm rotates against itself. "Oh, man!" Tears spring into my eyes.

"Don't move about," a voice says. "Lie down; your arm's broken; I feel much pain."

I look into the eyes of the most beautiful girl I've ever seen. Her eyes are like black jewels; her long, dark hair brushes across my face as she helps me lie flat. I'd think she was an angel except I'm pretty sure angels have blond hair and I don't think they say *aboot* instead of *about*. Wonder where she's from.

"I just want to close my eyes," I say.

She shakes her head. "Stay awake. You might have a concussion."

Yeah, or a hatchet through my head. "Where's my board?"

She looks around and stands up, and the floor creaks as she walks away from me.

"Oh, good," I say when she brings it back. "Not broken." Summer would bite without my skateboard. I'd be stuck sitting around the pool while Dad pecked out stories on his portable typewriter.

She lays my board by me and quickly stands. "I must go."

"Aw, man." I might start crying if I'm alone.

"They're coming," she says. "I'm not supposed to be here. Don't tell anyone."

Guests Prohibited.

I wince. She runs along the wall and disappears. I don't hear her, but now I hear voices coming up from the opposite direction. Uh-oh. One of them is my dad's.

5

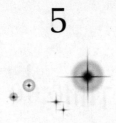

How the girl's heart had thundered when she revealed herself to the boy. His whimpering reminded her of pups struggling up the rocks, separated from their mothers. She could not but help him.

There was much risk in being seen, but what did this boy know of her? It was nothing to check on him. Her cousins had often helped others of his kind in troubled waters, taking pity on their flailing and thrashing; she could do no less.

Showing herself to the one called Allie Jo had been no accident. She had observed Allie Jo from afar for many days. The young girl had brown hair, not as dark as her own, and green eyes, the color of seawater. Often, Allie Jo poured black shells and yellow seeds into small wooden houses on poles; birds fluttered to the little shelters, eating greedily.

Once, after Allie Jo left, she'd scooped up some of the black shells for herself. They were crunchy, like winkles, her favorite snack.

6

Allie Jo

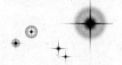

"Jinx, look, they're taking him away." I lean closer to the window frame of the fifth-floor nanny quarters, in the part I call the garden room. I'm hidden by the jacaranda tree; its ferny leaves are the perfect camouflage.

A bunch of tornadoes in the sixties knocked out all the windows up here. No one uses this floor, and no one has replaced any of the glass, which I think is actually an improvement to the place, since now the kudzu vines have crawled in and wrapped themselves along the walls and the ceiling. Sitting here is like sitting in an arbor. When the kudzu blooms, butterflies follow the vines right into the room and flit from flower to flower.

Leaning forward, I hear the paramedics' voices, but I can't make out what they're saying. When they were on the third floor, though, I heard everything they said. They asked that boy a whole bunch of questions, like "What year is it?" and "Who is the president?" That's how I know his name is Chase—it was the first question they asked him.

Chase looks small on the white gurney. Some kind of spongy thing is fitted around his head. "Where's his dad?" I say. I'd be scared to go in an ambulance alone.

Jinx is not curious about any of it, which is strange for a cat. She lies in a patch of sunlight hitting the strip of carpet I brought up here, holds up a black paw, and licks it. She's as comfy in this room as I am.

The walls of the floors below, the ones meant for tourists to see, are dressed in burgundy wainscoting with cream-colored chair rails a third of the way up. On top of the chair rail, the walls are covered in a striped wallpaper, cream and burgundy.

The wood is all original; that means it's the same wood they pulled up here on steam trains and horse-drawn wagons in 1887. Heart of pine and cedar—you'd learn that on the tour if you took it. The wallpaper has been replaced, but it's accurate for the time period. That little tidbit is straight from the tour too. People run their clean fingertips along the wallpaper, and after so many years, the oil from all their fingers ruins the wallpaper. It's kind of gross if you think about it.

There is no wallpaper up here in the nanny quarters. There's no chair rail either. No carpet. No glass. It sounds like this would be the worst place in the world, but it's actually the best. Downstairs is all dark and elegant; up here is all sunny and happy. There's a pink room, a yellow room, and a lavender room, and the hallway is painted green. Two window seats face each other on opposite ends of the quarters, and, boy, you can really get a nice breeze up here—you know, since there's no glass.

Wham! Wham! Paramedics shut the ambulance doors and slowly drive away. A little silver car follows close behind. I watch until I can't see them anymore.

"Well," I say, "they're gone." I breathe in, let out a big sigh. I've never seen an arm bent like that. "Maybe I shouldn't have chased him." I didn't want him to break his arm; I just wanted him to stop trespassing. I sure didn't expect to see him rolled out into an emergency vehicle. "Wonder why they don't put the sirens on?" I say out loud.

Jinx stares at me with her big, green eyes. The first time she dropped in from the window, I watched her sniff the kudzu. I didn't move a muscle; I didn't want to scare her away. When she kept coming back, I needed to call her something besides *Here, kitty, kitty.* I thought about names like Smoke or Shadow, but everyone with black cats uses those names. Not that I actually own Jinx. She started showing up here last summer, so I started feeding her.

I lean over and stroke her back. Her fur's warm from the sun. Closing her eyes and stretching, she purrs, and it's like a little motor rumbling inside of her. It rumbles into me and makes me feel good.

I haven't seen her for a couple of days. She comes and goes, but I always leave her something from breakfast and fill her water whether she's here or not.

She lifts her head and licks my hand with her scratchy tongue. Suddenly, she leaps up and swipes at a yellow butterfly moving lightly along the kudzu. A couple of monarchs flutter overhead.

Peaceful as it is, I keep seeing Chase flipping off that skateboard, the way it flew out from under his feet. Now that I replay it, I'm sure I heard a crunch when he snapped his bone. A little shudder runs through me. Maybe that crunch was his skateboard smacking the wall.

The skateboard—did he get it back? I can't remember that part. The least I can do is go get it for him. Before I stand, I pet Jinx one more time. She leans into my hand as I scratch between her ears; then she's swatting at that butterfly again. I hate leaving her alone up here, but I know she can take care of herself.

☾

The darkness of the fourth floor is almost depressing after the brightness and the liveliness on the fifth. I walk down the hall. The creaks are especially loud on the fourth and the third floors because neither of them has carpet or vines. The third floor doesn't really look any different from the fourth. It's dark and shadowy on account of some of the windows being boarded up.

A long time ago, one of the owners talked about knocking down the hotel, saying they could build a new, modern hotel or a strip mall in its place, but Hope raised such a fuss about The Meriwether being the heart and soul of the area's history that the owners instead sold it to an investment company, who sold it to another investment company, who sold it to the one who owns it now. I don't know what they're investing in when they still haven't bought new glass for the windows.

As I stroll down the hall, I scan its length for Chase's skateboard, but I don't see it. The floor groans and snaps under my feet; I don't think anything of it until I hear a scrape, and it's not coming from me.

Wood floors are not your friend when you're trying to be sneaky. The best thing to do is to walk on the edge, hugging the wall, like I do now. I listen for that scrape; it's coming from 312! I creep to the doorway and lay my fingers on the doorjamb like a spider stretching its legs toward its prey.

I whip myself around. "Gotcha!"

No one.

Still, I heard something, and it could be coming from

the closet or the gutted bathroom. Might be a squirrel. But I think it's a kid. I pick up a ratty old sneaker and hurl it into the closet. Nothing. I need to check the bathroom, but I don't see any more ammo.

"Allie Jo?" Mom's voice rises from the staircase. "Allie Jo?"

"I'm right here," I holler.

I lean against the wall, feel the ripples of peeling wallpaper ruffle against the back of my shirt. "You might as well come out," I say, crossing my arms. "My mom's coming up."

Nothing. Then a girl steps out of the closet and I whoop, practically jumping out of my skin. It's the girl from the springs! I am frozen to the spot. Her movements are so quiet and smooth, it's like she's floating. Her hair is silky, slipping over her shoulder. I forget to tell her that she is prohibited from being up here.

Erk! Aaar! Mom's footsteps. She's getting closer. "Allie Jo?"

The girl takes a step toward me, her mouth hinting at a smile.

My heart beats a little faster. She puts her finger up to her lips. *Shh,* she says, without making a sound at all. The footsteps are almost upon us. She puts her finger to her lips again and slips into the shadows of the closet.

"There you are!" Mom stops in the doorway, takes a

step in. "I've been looking all over for you. There's a girl downstairs I want you to meet. She's really nice and she'll be staying for the summer." She smiles. "I think she could use a friend."

What Mom really means is she thinks *I* could use a friend. I do have one, Melanie, but she's on vacation up north for the whole summer. A couple of girls who I did invite over, their moms wouldn't let them come because I live in this hotel. *Hotel rat* is what I hear behind my back, which, when you think of it, isn't even correct because I haven't ever seen a rat here, but I know an insult when I hear one.

Mom says people say mean things because they're jealous. I think people say mean things because they're mean.

What does it matter if you get your clothes from a secondhand store instead of from the mall? They probably came from the mall to begin with. And all the popular people have perms, but my hair is straight. That's okay, though—I don't want to look like a poodle.

I hate passing their lunch table during the school year. They giggle when I walk by, and once, when I was wearing my favorite checked shirt, one of them called out, *Hey, Allie Jo, did your mom make that shirt out of a tablecloth?* When I got home, I folded that shirt up very nicely and put it in the bottom of my dresser drawer.

They act like if your family doesn't have as much money as their family does, you're a nothing.

Who cares anyway—I'm busy enough without a bunch of girls getting in my way. I've got Clay and Chef, and there's Jinx to take care of, and my inspections—I really don't know if I have time for anyone else. Still, Mom's always pushing me to make friends even though I've explained to her I'm just fine with the way things are.

Like right now, for example. A secret girl is hiding in the closet, but Mom wants me to go downstairs to meet a regular girl. Mom steps into the room even farther, and my heart flares.

I block her path. "Okay!" I say. "Let's go!" Mom looks surprised at my enthusiasm. I'm surprised too. I don't know why—maybe it was the way she trusted me—but I'm keeping that girl's secret, whatever it is.

Mom loops her arm through mine. "Her name is Sophie and she's twelve." Close enough; I'm eleven. Mom rattles on and I feel torn as she pulls me out of the room. I take in the closet, but I see only darkness.

"Come on," Mom says, yanking me into the hall. "You can finish your inspection later. I think you'll like this girl."

7

Chase

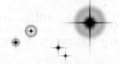

You'd think after all that, I'd get decent treatment—you know, sirens wailing, ambulance racing over curbs, medics rushing out of the ER, saying, *What've we got here?*

But no. The paramedics took their time loading me on a gurney and talking about their own skateboarding days while they pressed the button for the world's slowest elevator. No siren, and we stopped at every red light. Dad couldn't even ride in the ambulance with me because we needed the car to drive back to the hotel.

I don't know how long we wait at the emergency room or even if we wait. A bunch of people talk to Dad and keep saying *Hey, buddy* to me. I'm thirteen, not five, but whatever. The doctors explain what they're going to do and I'm all like, *Yeah, yeah, yeah*, because I'm thinking, *Just do it!* They decide I don't have a concussion. Then they give me some kind of shot and I feel it going from my left arm, flowing warmly through my veins, all the way through my body, until it reaches my head.

"Doing okay, buddy?" one of the doctors asks.

When I nod, I feel like I'm moving in slow motion, kind of woozy but good. My head lolls to the side and I watch Dad ask the doctor questions. I grin. He should sit down, relax. Everything's all right. He's a good guy, just works too hard, that's all. He needs a break. Look at him, writing stuff down even now. I snicker.

They turn to me. I flash them a peace sign.

It doesn't even hurt when, a few minutes later, the doctor manipulates my right arm so that the bones meet the right way. I am floating through space. Then they wrap, wrap, wrap up my arm a few inches past my elbow with long bandages; some are wet with plaster of paris. Cool.

As the cast sets, the doctor rattles off some rules. "No lotion or powder in the cast."

Check. No girlie stuff.

"Don't stick objects into the cast to scratch yourself."

Check. No objects.

"Do *not* get the cast wet."

What? I push through layers of puffy clouds. "What about swimming?"

The doctor shakes his head. "No swimming."

I knife through the clouds. "No swimming? What about the pool?" I glance at Dad, then back to the doctor.

He shakes his head again. "No swimming at all. You'll even need to be careful in the shower. If the cast gets wet, it'll break down, or mold or fungus could grow inside."

My mouth drops open. The clouds flit away. I turn to Dad, hoping he can help me out here. "Dad, the springs! What about snorkeling and all that?"

Dad exhales loudly and shakes his head.

"And you'll have to stay off that skateboard too. In fact, nothing with wheels," the doctor says. "We don't want you breaking the other arm." He gives what he probably thinks is a good-natured chuckle, then hands Dad a paper. "This goes over how to take care of the cast and what to look out for."

The last little bit of warm feeling leaves me. I can't believe this. I'm in Florida, just an hour from the ocean, only I can't swim in it; I'm stuck in a hotel with a pool I can't use, and now I can't even skateboard. What am I supposed to do? Play shuffleboard? Oh, yeah, I can't do that either—broke my shuffleboard arm.

☽

I'm sitting next to Dad in the Silver Bullet, the Camaro he and Mom bought before she left us. The Rusty Bullet, he should call it. *This thing's a beater, Dad. Why don't you get rid of it?* I've asked. *Nope.* He'd finger the New Hampshire Chevrolet sticker on it—that's where we lived when she was still with us.

Souvenirs are supposed to remind you of a good time you had somewhere. The Camaro is one big souvenir—it reminds Dad of good times with Mom. I have to look at photos to do that.

The seat belt's making my arm seriously uncomfortable. I unbuckle it.

"Put it back on." Dad doesn't look at me when he says it.

"Too uncomfortable."

"Just put it on," he says, sounding tired. Hey, I'm the one with the injury, remember?

I fumble with my left hand, trying to snap the buckle in, but it's not a one-arm job. Then the belt gets stuck and I try retracting it, which only makes it get stuck higher. I grit my teeth and yank on the belt.

Dad jerks his head at me. "What are you doing?"

"Trying to put on the seat belt like you said!" I pull on it. No go.

He shifts hands on the steering wheel and stretches his right hand over. "Well, let me help you if you can't get it."

"I don't need your help!" I go into crazy mode,

retracting the belt and yanking it over and over again until, finally, it comes loose and I pull it down. But I still can't make the connection; the buckle keeps flopping. My lips smash together as I try and fail one more time. I breathe hard through my nose. A trickle of sweat runs down my right arm and into the cast. Great. My body goes rigid: one arm frozen into a right angle; the other arm frozen in position holding the seat belt.

Dad reaches over and holds the buckle still. I push the seat belt in and it snaps into place.

We ride in silence to the hotel.

8

Allie Jo

Knit one, purl two. Or at least I thought that's what knitting would be. I loop the yarn around the needle and try to pull it back.

"Oops! You dropped a stitch." Sophie lays her own needles down and takes the ones she's lent me.

We're sitting in the parlor next to the grand staircase that separates us from the front-desk area. I happen to think it's an excellent sitting area, good for reading, for thinking, and especially for spying on every single guest that comes to check in, but since there's not much going on today, knitting is okay too.

When Sophie and I first met yesterday, I was a little put off after Mom dragged me away from the third floor and that girl hiding in the closet. Also, I saw how pretty Sophie was. In my experience, pretty girls are usually mean, like Jennifer Jorgensen from school—that's why you have to avoid them. But the first thing Sophie said was how lucky I was to be living here, so I shucked the chip right off my shoulder and crunched it under my feet.

Sophie hands my knitting back to me. "There you go!"

Raising the needle up, I examine a few rows that weren't there before. You'd think a person might get mad, someone doing their project for them, but I'm glad. Sophie said I should start off with a scarf, and she wondered if it ever gets cold in Florida, but I said a scarf would do just fine, since I saw it was nothing but straight lines. Easy as pie.

Boy, was I wrong. You've got to have nimble fingers to knit, and Sophie's pale fingers fly with the yarn. She's making a scarf, too, but hers has patterns she knits right into it. Still, I'm happy with mine. She let me pick from her bundles of yarn, and I pulled out a ball of the most shimmery green I've ever seen.

My best friend, Melanie, doesn't knit. She likes to watch TV and go swimming, but only if there's no one else in the pool. This is on account of she's kind of what you might call—well, I don't like to say anything bad about her; she's my best friend and all—but the kids at school call her Shamu, so now you know what I'm talking about, but I didn't say it myself.

If I get really good at knitting, I'll teach Melanie how

to do it when she gets back from up north. I hate that she's gone all summer. Not only is she my best friend, she's my closest friend, and I really mean that—she's the only girl from school who lives in bike-riding distance. I don't count Jennifer Jorgensen and her little followers; they don't live too far, but they think they're so big because they're one grade ahead of me. When Melanie gets back, we'll knit ourselves all kinds of fancy stuff and everyone else will be jealous.

Where'd you get that? Jennifer Jorgensen will ask, eyeing my scarf.

I'll toss it around my neck. *It's one of kind,* I'll say, and Melanie and I will walk off airily.

"Oh, um . . . ," Sophie says. "I think you dropped a couple of stitches."

"Oh!" I hand the little bit I've done to her, determined to pay more attention. "You're really good at this. How long have you been knitting?"

Her eyes fastened to the needles, she goes, "I don't know, a long time. My grandma taught me." She hands my scarf back to me, which is about two inches long now. "She wanted me to have something to do, since I stay indoors a lot." She picks up her needles. "I have allergies."

"Allergies!" I drop another stitch. Putting my knitting in my lap, I glance at her. She doesn't look like she has a disease or anything. Well, maybe she is kind of slim and sort of pale, but I expect that's from being indoors all the time. "That's terrible!"

She shakes her head. "It's not bad. My parents are like experts when it comes to medicine, pollen counts, and allergens. When I was little, my mom kept my stuffed animals in bags."

"Bags?" They wouldn't have been able to breathe. Sure, I know they don't need to, but when you're little, you think they do. That's why you also feed them.

"To keep the dust off." She looks at me. "But none of my stuff is in bags now. I mainly get stuck indoors a lot."

I think about that and nod. "You'll be stuck indoors anyway," I say. "This is the rainy season." When she looks confused, I explain. "There're two seasons in Florida: hot, and hot and rainy." Then I say dramatically, "You're in the jungle now!"

She takes her eyes off her knitting and looks at me wide-eyed.

I like a good audience. "Yes," I hiss. "Alligators! Fire ants! Lizards!" Melanie sometimes hangs lizards by their jaws from her earlobes, trying to gross me out. It works.

"What about monkeys?" she asks. "Monkeys live in the jungle."

"Monkeys!" I nod. "But not here. In Silver Springs. They made the Tarzan movies there a long time ago and the monkeys escaped. Now they're all wild, living in the tree-tops."

"Wow!"

Of course this makes me like her more. I like anyone who appreciates what I've got to say. Plus, look how nice she is, sharing her good yarn with me and everything.

"Welcome to Florida," I say with a big smile, then quote the slogan: "The rules are different here."

9

Chase

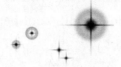

Guests Prohibited. Yeah, right. I step over the cord and keep going. The way I see it, I have full rein now that I'm stuck with this stupid cast. It took me so long to get dressed today that Dad offered to zip up my shorts. *No way,* I said. *I can do it myself.* He hung around until after lunch, but then he had to interview the guy at the bungee jumping place.

Third floor looks the same as before, except someone skinny is walking down the hall. Ha! It's that girl who yelled at me—Allie Jo, I think her name is. That's what I *think* I heard when everyone was buzzing around me and my broken arm. I slip real quiet into the first room, lean toward the doorway, and moan like a ghost.

She gasps. Aw, man, too funny.

I wait a few seconds, then, "Woo-oo-ooo, woo-oo-ooo!"

Silence. I'm cracking myself up. I give her a minute, then lean out again. "Woo-oo—"

"Gotcha!" She whirls around the door frame and we bonk heads.

"OW!" I rub my head. Better than letting her know she scared me.

"Oh, my gosh, are you okay?" She holds both hands by her mouth. After I nod, she straightens up. "You need to get off this floor. You're not allowed to be here." She leans back into the hallway and scans it nervously.

The corner of my lip pulls up and I stand back from her. "If I can't be up here, you can't be up here."

"I live here," she says like she owns the place.

"So do I." I lift my chin. "For the summer anyway."

She opens her mouth, clamps it shut, and crosses her arms. In a loud, booming voice, she shouts, "You can't be sneaking around up here!" Then she does another quick scan of the hallway.

"Why're you barking at me?" I yell. "Why do you keep looking down the hall?"

Her head gives a sudden jerk. I make a move to cut through the doorway, but she tries to block me.

I grin. Then I fake left and bolt right.

"Hey!"

She pounds down the hall after me, but I've got a big head start. I turn around and jog backward. "Come on! Catch me!"

But she's not laughing. Her face looks panicked. When she catches up to me, I swear she's blinking back tears. Way to go, Chase.

This is how you can sometimes apologize: don't actually say you're sorry; just act like everything's normal and keep talking even if the other person ignores you. It works. They usually get tired of being mad at you.

"What are you doing up here anyway?" I ask her.

If looks could kill, I'd be under a headstone.

I gesture with my cast. "You want to sign it?" Everyone likes to sign casts.

Except maybe her. Gamma rays emit from her eyes. She purses her lips.

"Come on," I say. "I can't go around with just D-A-D."

She smirks. "What about M-O-M?"

I don't let that break my stride as we head down the stairs. "M-O-M isn't H-E-R-E," I say. Then I quickly add, "She's visiting some other people."

We step around the banister to the front desk and she rings the bell. *Ding, ding, ding.*

The sandy-haired guy steps out from the office, his face expectant until he sees Allie Jo. He puts his hands on the desk and raises an eyebrow.

"Hey, Clay!" she says. "Got any markers?"

Clay cracks a lopsided smile, opens a drawer, and hands her a box. "What are you up to now?" he asks.

"I'm signing his cast," she says, rooting through the box.

"Yeah, I heard about that," he says, and he glances at me. "I skateboard down at the park. Some wicked rails down there. But if you're looking for something really exciting, you should try skiboarding."

The marker squeaks over my cast as Allie Jo signs it.

"Not this summer," I say with true regret.

Allie Jo stands back. "All done!"

I look down. "Pink!" *Allie Jo Jackson* in huge bubble gum pink letters. I could throttle her.

Clay laughs. "Too late, dude—that stuff's permanent!"

I give Allie Jo a murderous look, but she snickers, tossing the marker back in the box.

I can't let that pink dominate my cast. "Hey Clay, want to sign it?"

So when we leave the front desk, my cast is looking better, and by better I mean more populated—I don't mean pink.

"I could just color over your signature," I say to her. I have no idea where we're walking to; I'm just following her. "Dudes shouldn't wear pink."

"Pink is just red with white in it," she says. "Why do boys always make such a big deal about that?"

She stops in front of the dining room and grabs a peppermint out of a bowl. "You want one?" she asks, grabbing another before I can even nod.

I grasp one end of the plastic with my casted fingertips, then try to twist it open with my other hand. After a few seconds, Allie Jo takes it from me, opens it, and hands me the unwrapped candy.

I hate feeling helpless. "Thanks."

She shrugs and skips ahead of me, turning into a dark corridor with some stairs. As she goes up, I stand at the bottom. I can't see all the way up, but I can sure smell the mildew.

She turns around at the first landing. "You know how to play rummy?"

"Yeah." Everyone knows how to play rummy.

"Well, come on then."

Ha! Looks like I'm not *prohibited* after all.

10

Allie Jo

"Oh, my gosh!" Chase says when I lead him into the nanny quarters.

I brought him up the service stairs because I didn't think he'd manage the secret nanny staircase on account of it being so narrow. Besides, I don't know if I want to give away all my secrets.

As we pass down the hallway, the flutter of wings beats over our heads.

"Duck!" Chase yells, and we both drop as a bird swoops over our heads and floats down the hall.

"No—seagull," I say.

He pinches his eyebrows together; then he gets it. "Ha, ha."

I've got a better one. "If a gull from the sea is a seagull, what is a gull from the bay?"

He falls for it. "A baygull."

"Right! A bagel."

He shakes his head.

As I lead him into the garden room, a squirrel skitters out the window and down the long jacaranda branch. A black swallowtail flits right past Chase's nose and I watch his gaze follow it to the vines along the ceiling.

"This place is wild!" he says.

"Yup." If I was wearing suspenders, I'd snap them. "That vine's called kudzu," I tell him. "It grows a foot a day—that's half an inch every hour."

He opens his mouth real big and crunches his eyebrows down. "No way!"

"Yes way!" I say, pushing a tendril away from me. "That's why we don't leave dogs sleeping in the yard overnight. The kudzu would have them covered and tied up by morning. You don't believe me, just look out your window when you're driving. You'll see all kinds of things under that kudzu now that you know about it." I look off to the side. "Yessir, the vine that ate the South."

"Whoa," he murmurs.

As I mentioned before, I do like an appreciative audience. But when I turn to him, I see it isn't my story he's reacting to; it's my collection.

Whenever I find something worth keeping, I bring it up here and add it to my collection. Stuff that looks expensive I turn in to Lost and Found, which Clay keeps in a box under the front desk, but even that stuff gets passed on after thirty days, and I get first pick. You wouldn't believe what people leave behind: wedding rings, cameras, shoes . . .

"A tape recorder!" Chase exclaims. He bends down and grabs it. "Let's record something."

"No!" I swipe it away from him and sit on the carpet. "It's already got something recorded on it."

This tape recorder sat in Lost and Found for two months before Clay let me have it. It belonged to a girl. I know this because the cassette inside is marked *Isabelle, April 1983*—four years ago. It's kind of like a diary, and she sings nursery rhymes on it too. Sometimes, I sit up here and listen to Isabelle. If she ever came back, we'd probably be best friends because I already know everything about her.

"Listen." I press the Play button.

Isabelle's voice comes out loud and clear:

> *My body lies over the ocean,*
> *My body lies over the sea.*
> *My body lies over the ocean,*
> *Oh, bring back my body to me.*

"That's supposed to be *Bonnie*, not *body*!" Chase says.

"Shh!" Gosh, you can tell by listening that Isabelle was

only about five or six when she made this tape. It's okay if she gets a word wrong.

> *Bring back,*
> *Bring back,*
> *Oh, bring back my body to me-ee-ee.*
> *Bring back,*
> *Bring back,*
> *Oh, bring back my body to me.*

I click off the tape recorder and glance at him. "There's a lot more," I say, but I can tell he's not that interested in Isabelle.

That's okay. I know that she went to Disney World and wished she could spend the night in the Swiss Family Treehouse. Her baby sister, Cassie, giggled a lot. One time, Isabelle put the microphone right by Cassie's mouth and Cassie laughed and laughed. I grin every time I get to that part. And sometimes she recorded her older sister, Karen—a *teenager*.

But boys don't care about sisters and secrets.

I push the tape recorder back and get the cards out. I beat Chase at two hands of rummy; then he gets lucky and plays a set of queens, a set of threes, four-five-six of hearts, and discards a card. If I didn't see it with my own eyes, I'd accuse him of cheating.

Then I do a card trick, a cool one where I make his card come to the top.

"How'd you do that?" His face is one big question mark.

I just smile and put the cards back into the box.

11

Chase

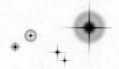

Dad and I are watching a video he rented called *Teen Wolf*. It's about this high school guy who's an okay basketball player until he turns into a werewolf—then he's suddenly the most popular guy on campus. And his dad's a werewolf too. But his mom's dead.

I'd rather have a dead mother than one who ran off. If your mom's dead, people feel sorry for you and the other moms treat you like an adopted son. But if they know your mom up and left, all they do is get really fake and pry for information: *Where does she live? Do you see her often? What does she do for a living?*

Why? I want to ask. *Are you planning to run off too?* I just want them to shut up. And besides, I don't know where she is. The last picture of her with me, I'm toddling away and she's laughing, grabbing me by the back of my diaper.

Yeah, a dead mother would be better.

Scott, the teen wolf, is getting ready for the final game of the season when a big snore rumbles from the other hotel bed. I toss a pillow, hitting Dad in the stomach.

He springs up. "Huh? What?" Dazed and confused.

"Can't hear the TV," I say. "You sound like a train."

Dad smirks. "I'm kinda hungry."

We ate supper a couple of hours ago. Nothing like stone crab; definitely better than the orange macaroni and cheese I make from the box at home.

"I'm kinda hungry too," I say, thinking of the dessert menu at the hotel's dining room. Hmm, chocolate cheese-cake or the Dusty Miller Sundae? *The boy leaned his head, perplexed by the decision he must now make.* Oh, that's good. I'll have to use that line in a story for school.

Dad tosses his wallet to me. "Go get us a snack from the vending machine."

☾

I'm looking for some microwave popcorn, but the second-floor vending machine's empty, so I head on down to the first floor's machine. Do I want regular, extra butter, or cheese?

It's gonna be either D2 or D3 because regular's boring, I think, when a girl's voice pops up behind me.

"Um, excuse me?"

I turn around. Huge, blue eyes. That's the first thing I notice. Then her blond hair. Pink lips.

I smile and stare like a doofus, forgetting to speak.

She smiles. "Do you mind if I just get something? I already know what I want."

"Go ahead" are the witty words I say. I move to the side—what a bonehead—and watch as she presses D2.

Thump! She grabs it, says thanks over her shoulder, and bounces down the hall.

Hey, what's your name? I'm getting popcorn too! Movie night, huh? All the things I could have said now roll into my brain. Oh, well. I hit D2 and head back up to the room.

When I get there, the credits are rolling.

"Oh!" Dad holds up the remote. "Want me to rewind? I wasn't paying attention."

I rattle off the plastic and stick our popcorn in the microwave. "Let me guess—he makes the winning shot, defeats his enemy, and gets the girl." The kernels begin to pop.

"More or less," Dad says.

Rat-a-tat-tat. The kernels fire off, bursting in the bag.

"Rewind," I say. Blue eyes and blond hair. I settle in for a happy ending.

12

Allie Jo

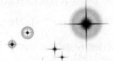

The next morning, I catch a glimpse of someone tall with long, black hair at the back of the dining room. Half jumping out of my seat, I knock into the table, then watch as one of our cooks opens the door to the kitchen, his long, black hair swinging in a ponytail.

"What?" Mom asks, holding her coffee cup in two hands. We're just finishing our breakfast.

I sink into my chair. "Nothing," I say. "Thought I saw someone I knew."

Mom suddenly sits straighter. "There's someone you know!"

I twist in my seat. "Sophie!" I call out across the dining room. She's with her parents. I wave them over.

"Allie Jo!" Mom sets her cup down. "Don't yell—you'll disturb the other guests."

A bunch of old ladies take up three tables and I can spot the hearing aids from here. The only other guests are a couple with a baby in a high chair, and the baby's making a lot more noise than I am.

"Hello, Becky!" Mrs. Duran greets Mom. Then she turns to me. "And how are you today, Allie Jo?"

She has kind blue eyes with crinkles at the sides.

I smile at her. "I'm fine." I like her because she's Sophie's mom and I like Sophie.

Mom invites them to join us; then the fathers start to make a big production of pulling tables together, since we're at a four-top.

"No, no!" I say, and quickly get up, grabbing my plate and fork. "I'm done."

"Are you sure?" Mrs. Duran asks.

The moment they sit down, they'll talk about *Oh, this weather!* and *Did you see those gas prices?* and other boring stuff, like on the news. "Yes, I'm sure," I say.

"Can I come with you?" Sophie asks in a rush.

"Honey," Mrs. Duran says, "you haven't eaten."

Sophie makes a face and touches her middle. "I have a stomachache."

They decide that Sophie will meet them in their room at eleven thirty to go to a museum. Until then, Mrs. Duran says, "Have a good time!" She pulls Sophie in for a quick peck on the cheek.

"Mo-om!" Sophie steals a quick glance at me.

"Don't worry," I say. "My mom does the same thing."

Sophie smiles. "I'm almost a teenager, you know."

"Me too!" I'll be thirteen in one year and seven and a half months.

As we pass the kitchen, I push open the swinging door and spot Chef. "Got any tuna fish?"

He hands me a little to-go container already filled. "Enjoy," he says.

"Thanks, Chef Boyardee," I say in a super-sweet voice.

He lifts a spatula and waves me away.

Sophie looks positively repulsed when I turn from the kitchen with my little container. "You eat tuna fish for breakfast?"

"Brain food," I say, turning left out of the dining room. "Haven't you ever heard that about fish?"

She follows me down the hall. "Well, yeah, but—"

"Students who eat a protein-filled breakfast score higher on tests and are more creative in everything they do." That's in my school handbook.

I look both ways, then duck into the service tower. "You coming?"

"Where are you going?" she calls from the hallway.

I gesture with the tuna fish. "I've got to feed my cat."

13

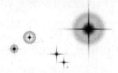

The scent woke the girl up, filled her being. Fish! Her stomach growled in recognition. She sat up from the floor, letting the blanket fall from her. She'd discovered this small room last night, a room with shelves and blankets. From them, she'd made something of a nest for herself and had slept well. Perhaps that had something to do with the door. It blocked people out.

But it didn't block out that wonderful fragrance! She followed it through a narrow door and up a staircase. She could hear voices—Allie Jo and another.

She thought to dash back to her nest, but hunger demanded she go forward. She must eat. The stairs ended at a place with lots of rooms. Faint notions came to her, but the growling of her stomach drowned them out.

Suddenly footsteps and talking neared her! Her heart,

usually slow and controlled, pumped up. She tucked herself into an alcove, waiting until they passed.

Yes, it was Allie Jo, and a girl, fair and light. The air was pleasant around the girl she hadn't met, but she did not wish to reveal herself. She must be sure it was safe. Waiting in the alcove, she stilled herself, breathing slowly.

Laughter came from the other room, but the laughter of many, not just two. Her heart leaped. How did she miss these others? Was she losing her senses?

Then there was much sneezing, and the footsteps neared her. Again they passed by her—only the two of them—and descended the stairs.

She tarried in the alcove, straining her ears for the other voices she'd heard, yet none sounded. The smell of fish drifted teasingly under her nose. She could deny her stomach no more and swept through the rooms toward the scent.

Ah, but what curious thing was this—a black creature with fur, devouring the very food she sought. She drew near cautiously, for she had never seen such a being. She sat on the floor and watched it. Perhaps it would leave some for her.

14

Chase

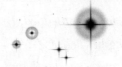

This is what the wood floor sounds like: *Irrp! Crack! Reee-raw.* I make that last sound by slowly stepping on this one spot and lifting my foot again. *Reee-raw, reee-raw.* And that's not the only noise either. Pipes line the ceiling—they're in the rooms too—and something's clinking in them. If I weren't thirteen, I might think it was a ghost.

I'm walking down the hallway, fingering the cuff of my cast. Feels like there're ants in there, it's so itchy. Dad's gone to cover a waterskiing attraction, but first we went out for lunch.

Usually, I like to stick my hand out the window and let the wind whip it around, but I didn't think the cast was made for winds at sixty-five miles per hour. So I day-dreamed and stared out the window. All of a sudden, I saw it.

"Kudzu!" I hollered. I couldn't believe it—it covered everything: telephone poles, billboards, whole sections of woods. Allie Jo was right.

"What?" Dad yelled back. We zoomed down the highway. He probably couldn't focus on the scenery.

"Nothing!" Kudzu was not worth a car crash.

After lunch, Dad secured me in the room—*Sorry, bud*—and left.

I rake the top of the cast; it's driving me crazy. I stick my fingers in to scratch, but I can't squeeze them in far enough. The doc had said, *Tap on the cast if you're itchy.* Yeah, right. I'm doing Morse code, but it ain't working.

I head out of the room. Dim chandeliers cast just enough light to see the cobwebs hanging from them. I have a crazy urge to jump up and swing from them. I could swing from light to light, Tarzan of the hotel. The sounds from televisions seep under the gaps of several doorways, but other than that, no sign of life.

My arm's on fire with this itching. I jog downstairs, through the main hallway, and straight toward the front desk. They gotta have something to help me with this crazy itch. But just before I reach the desk, I hit one of those displays with all the attraction flyers. *Wax Museum! Experience the Light of Flight! Learn to Water Ski!*

This last one is the one I pull out. That's where Dad is today, where I would have been except for my stupid broken arm. Fumbling with my left hand, I stick one edge of the flyer into my right hand and stretch the brochure open. I look at a picture of a guy being pulled on water skis by an overhead rope tow. Forget it—I don't get to be that guy, not this summer. I take a deep breath. Trying to fold the flyer back up is impossible. I crumple it instead and leave it on top of the display.

"Um, excuse me?"

The vending-machine girl! I slip into doofus mode.

She smiles. "Um . . . I thought maybe you could use this?" She waves a knitting needle.

My brain's gone dead. I'm not making the connection. I tilt my head like a dog that doesn't understand something.

"You know," she says, "for your arm—to scratch your arm. You keep scratching your cast."

"Oh, yeah—yeah, that would be great." It's great that I can talk again. This girl is so pretty. I take the needle from her and slide it under the cast. "Aw, man." I shake my head. "You don't know how good that feels."

She laughs and I do too. Then we don't say anything.

"Hi, Chase!" Allie Jo walks up behind her. She's holding knitting needles too; some kind of green thing hangs from one of them. "This is Sophie. Can she sign your cast?"

Sophie's mouth drops open and she turns. "Allie Jo!"

"No! It's okay!" I say too loudly. "You can sign it."

Allie Jo grins at Sophie, handing off her knitting. "I'll go get a marker."

"Not pink!" I yell after her.

Allie Jo comes back with a blue marker, and when Sophie signs the cast, she lays one hand on it and writes with the other. Her hair tickles my fingers. She's so close, I can smell her strawberry lip gloss.

"Sophie," she says, and gives me a strawberry smile.

I smile back, feeling something like a current between us.

"Nice handwriting," Allie Jo says. She talks in capital letters—loud and important.

I like how Sophie dotted the *i*, a circle over big, loopy letters. She had to write her name on the inner side of the cast because *Allie Jo Jackson* takes up the entire top of it, and *Clay* and *Dad* are on the other side. That's okay, though, because Sophie's side of the cast is closest to me.

"How's your arm feeling?" Sophie asks.

"Still broken!" Good one, Chase.

They tehee for a moment, then Sophie goes, "No, I mean . . . um—"

"You've got her needle stuck in your cast," Allie Jo says.

"Oh!" Doofus. I slide the needle out and hand it to

Sophie. "Sorry about that." I feel a hangdog expression creeping over my face like kudzu.

"No big deal." She gives me a huge smile. "You can use it again if you need to."

Hmm. I foresee an itchy arm in my future.

15

Allie Jo

"And this is the service tunnel. At the turn of the century, most of our guests traveled by train or stagecoach and stayed on for several months. Naturally, they had large wardrobes to pack."

We're standing in the entrance to the tunnels that crisscross under the hotel. Mom's giving her tour, which, this being a Tuesday, has a small turnout: me, Chase, Sophie, and Ryan and Nicholas, the two brothers I babysit. Nicholas is seven and Ryan is four, and they live in the family suite on the first floor since their parents work here too.

I stand beside Mom, facing our audience. As she speaks, I mouth every word she says; I know the whole thing by heart. If they pay attention, they'll learn a lot of stuff.

"After the guests disembarked, porters ran out to unload the trunks, and there were many of them, as you— Allie Jo?" She turns to me. "What are you doing?"

"Nothing. Please continue." This is fun.

"There were many of them, as you can imagine, and they were quite heavy. The porters loaded them onto handcarts and pulled them up the lawn to this service tower."

I gesture around with my hands like she does. Nicholas snickers.

Mom gives me that mom look. I make sure to look innocent.

"Servants were not to be seen back then, so, as you can see, these tunnels have paths leading to every corner of the hotel— Allie Jo, what are you doing?" She whips around, one hand on her hip, a little smile on her lips.

"She's saying your words!" Nicholas yells. Ryan bursts out laughing, and I see Sophie's and Chase's mouths struggling to keep straight.

"Well, you know the tour as well as I do," she says. She looks at our little group. "Ladies and gentlemen"—she gestures with her hand—"your new tour guide."

"Thank you, Mom." I bow as Mom steps aside.

I swing open a heavy cedar door. "You will notice the brick-lined rooms on either side. The small one on your left was the first one built. It was the icebox. It's been gut-ted, but you can still tell by its pantry shape how it might have been used."

Sophie raises her hand.

"Yes? In the back?" I ask.

Chase guffaws.

Sophie steals a glance at him, then looks at me. "You mean like a refrigerator?"

"Yes. Huge blocks of ice were carried in and stored in there with food. The hotel became so popular, a second room was needed.

"Now, our young men were off fighting in the First World War, and then the Great Depression hit. This was also the time of Prohibition."

Mom raises her hand and speaks before I call on her. "What does that mean?"

"Good question," I say, then direct my answer to Chase and Sophie.

"Prohibition is when the government wouldn't let people drink alcohol. But these were times when people needed relief the most, so Mr. Meriwether built the sec-ond room really big"—I look around the way Mom does at this point, as if she can't risk the wrong person hearing the next part, and I stage-whisper—"and he turned it into a speakeasy." I straighten up and let that sink in.

Only they just stare at me. "Don't you know what a speakeasy is?"

They shake their heads.

"It's a place where people could come and drink and forget their troubles. This is where Mr. Meriwether met Mrs. Meriwether. She was already married, but once she spotted Mr. Meriwether, that was it—love at first sight."

Chase's features pull together and he frowns.

"They'd meet here in secret until her husband found out and divorced her. You see that porthole, that little window? Well, the doorman inside the speakeasy would slide it open to make sure the person knocking wasn't a policeman. Mr. Meriwether used it to make sure it wasn't the husband on the other side."

Sophie gasps with pleasure, her face lit up, but Chase looks positively stormy.

"I wish the husband had beaten the door down and punched the guy out," he says.

"That wouldn't have happened," I say, wondering a little at his remark. "The old chief of police himself was usually in there, trying to win some of Mr. Meriwether's money at the poker table."

"Oh, my gosh!" Sophie says, which, of course, is the correct response.

I look at Mom and she smiles back. I've done pretty

well, I think. I let her take over again, this being as far as she ever leads anyone into the tunnel. We go up the stairs and she shows us the framed black-and-white photos of long-ago movie stars sitting on the veranda or, in Clark Gable's case, eating The Meriwether's Famous Blueberry Pancakes in the Emerald Dining Room.

Mom ends the tour at the front desk and gives everyone, me included, a Meriwether magnet, then says goodbye, what a good tour group we were, and all that stuff.

Ryan tugs on my shirt. He cups his hand to whisper, waiting until I bend. "What's wrong wif his arm?" His breath is hot and moist on my ear.

"Fractured femur," I say. It's the only bone word I know.

"That's a leg bone," Chase says. He turns to Ryan. "I broke my arm."

"Oh." Ryan's mouth puckers. "Did it hurt?"

"It hurt a lot. You want to sign my cast?"

Both boys shriek and jump. Instead of dinging for Clay, I get the markers myself and give one to each boy. Ryan knows how to write his name, and it turns out pretty well for a four-year-old. Nicholas takes great care in writing his name.

I ask Sophie and Chase, "How'd you like the tunnel?" For most people, the tunnel and the speakeasy are their favorite parts of the tour.

"I don't think you guys should be talking about people leaving their husbands," Chase spouts. "You tell it like it's a real love story."

I stare at him in surprise. "I thought you liked the tour."

"I didn't like that part," he says.

Sophie's fingers press against her lips. "I thought it was kind of interesting."

"Well, it's not interesting to me," he says. "There's nothing interesting about that, okay?"

Most people like the tour. "What's the matter with you?" I say. I am surprised and a little annoyed with his lack of appreciation.

He glances up at me, and I swear, his face looks all lost for a second, then he pulls it together and says, "Nothing. I didn't mean that. It was a good tour."

I stare at him. "Well!" That's all I can think of. If I was done knitting my scarf, I'd whirl it around my neck and storm off.

16

Chase

After the tour, Sophie has to split for lunch with her parents, and Nicholas and Ryan's mom comes to get them. I'm kind of hungry too. I finger the dollar bills from Dad in my pocket and think about that vending machine by the game room.

Strands of Allie Jo's hair cling to her forehead. You know how people say, *It's not the heat; it's the humidity*? Well, it's true. "Let's go to my house," she says. "I'm hungry."

"That's okay," I say. "I'm not really hungry." I'm kind of leery about going to other people's houses. Once you're in, if things don't go well, you're trapped. Besides, I point out, "I thought you lived here."

"I do live here and I know you're hungry. I heard your stomach growling."

Objection! I think to myself. *The opposition is using*

evidence not declared by this court! Still, her kitchen probably has something better than the bag of pretzels I was planning.

Her house turns out to be a suite above the hotel's restaurant. I thought it would be like the room Dad and I are in, but it looks like a regular home once you get inside: living room, kitchen, hallway. There are pictures everywhere: Mom, Dad, and Allie Jo at the beach; Mom, Dad, and Allie Jo with Mickey Mouse; Dad holding a baby— must be Allie Jo. We have pictures like that too, in a box in the basement. Dad thinks I don't know he looks at them, but when I pull the box out, the pictures are in a different order from how I left them.

"Mo-om!" Allie Jo calls out as we enter.

A man comes from another room. Her dad, who is also the manager. Hope I don't get a lecture about obeying the rules.

"Hey, Allie Jo." He pulls her in for a quick hug. "You're Chase, right? Recognized you by the cast."

My calling card.

"You're just in time for lunch. You eat yet, Chase?"

I shake my head.

Allie Jo follows him into the kitchen. I don't want to, but I follow her. "Will you make us grilled cheese?" she asks, uncapping some juice and pouring it into two cups.

He waves a spatula. "Boom! You're grilled cheese."

Now I see where she gets her sense of humor. Still, it's so corny that it's funny.

Allie Jo's leaning on the island, sipping her juice. I gulp mine down. I'm waiting for her to head into another room, like I would, but she stays there, even after her juice is gone.

"Where's Mom?"

Apparently, her mom is running errands. Her dad starts talking about Taste of Hope, the festival coming up in a few weeks.

"Should be a big to-do," he says, flipping the grilled cheese. He's making three of them. "Chef's already working up the trays."

Allie Jo's face lights up. "Ooooh! I can't wait!" She turns to me. "It's, like, the biggest thing in the summer, and at night it's July Fourth."

Confused, I ask, "Isn't it July Fourth during the day too?"

"Of course, silly—everyone comes out for the festival, and then stays for the fireworks."

Her dad puts the grilled cheeses on plates, dumps some chips on them, and sets the plates on the island. "Order up!"

"Thanks, Dad," Allie Jo says, picking up a plate.

I pick up a plate too and follow her to the table. "Yeah, thanks."

"No problem," he says, flipping the spatula like a drumstick. "It's my only specialty." Then he sits with us at the table.

It is grilled just right. "Mmm, good," I say.

Allie Jo looks at her dad. "Tell him what you call them."

He looks a little embarrassed but puffs out his chest and says, "Golden brown crispy with melted cheese in between—Jackson style."

They pretend-argue over who invented the golden brown crispy part, then move on to other things. He asks me questions, like what grade am I going into, do I play basketball, what can I do on a skateboard, and the weird thing is that he's listening, really listening. He's not lost in his own world, editing stories in his head. When my dad "listens," I can practically see the typewriter ribbon ticking across his eyeballs.

"Your dad's pretty cool," I tell Allie Jo after lunch. "So's your mom." We sit on their sundeck. The view isn't the best—it overlooks the top of the restaurant. Vents that look like chefs' hats hum with blades spinning inside them. Different food smells float up here, but I'm already satisfied by the grilled cheese.

"Yeah, they are pretty cool." She slouches in the lawn

chair and puts her feet up on the railing. "What's your mom like?"

I shrug.

"Oh, yeah," she says, "visiting other people. When's she coming here?"

I don't feel like making up a story. I take a deep breath. "She's not coming here," I say without looking at Allie Jo. "She's gone."

"Gone?"

I cock my head and look at her sideways.

Her face shifts from confusion to shock. Then she covers her mouth. "Oh! That's terrible!"

"Not dead," I say. "Just . . . gone."

"Like, what do you mean? Are they divorced? Don't you see her anymore? Don't you know where she is?"

"She's just gone, okay?" I slam my back against the chair. A seagull lands on the deck by me but leaves when he sees I have nothing for him. "No big deal," I say in a quieter voice. "Okay?"

Allie Jo looks at me like she's reading for comprehension. What does she know anyway? Her mom probably calls her "honey" and her dad's in the kitchen getting ready to make us ice-cream sundaes.

She starts to say something, but I cut her off. "I think I better get going."

"Oh." She looks down.

I get up. "Thanks for lunch," I call out to her dad as we pass the kitchen. I head for the door and turn around. "Hey, Allie Jo, guess what?"

Her eyes become alert. "What?"

"I have to return my butt to Kmart," I say. "Mine's cracked."

She snickers.

I'd fit right in here.

17

Allie Jo

I've finished my blueberry pancakes and got a double portion of tuna for Jinx. I don't know what's gotten into her lately—she's eating more than she ever used to.

I snitch a peppermint on my way past the hostess stand, and when no one's looking, I cross the hall, walk a few paces, and press on the chair rail, which is just a piece of wood trim. Strolling down the hall, you'd never notice the secret panel that opens up to the nanny staircase. It looks like every other part of the wall, with the wainscoting and chair rail, but press down, and—*voila!*—secret staircase.

I slip in real quick, shutting the door with my foot.

The grand staircase is wide and elegant, with curved handrails and turned balusters. The reason it's so wide is— well, you have to think about those turn-of-the-century ladies wearing those big hoop dresses while trying to get through the place. In fact, it's on account of those ladies that the stairs were built with huge landings between flights. Those poor ladies squeezed into corsets so tight, they could barely breathe, yet they had to walk up and down these stairs gasping for breath and no air-conditioning on top of it. That's why fainting couches were available on each landing. And they were used mightily too.

The staircase I'm in is the secret nanny staircase. You might think this staircase would be wide too, since the nannies were ladies, or girls, and they wore hoop skirts and corsets too, and on top of that, they had a trail of children with them at all times.

But no, this staircase is narrow and dark. The landings are only big enough for you to turn up to the next flight of stairs. There're a few lights in here now—though most of the bulbs burned out a long time ago—but the nannies had to find their way by oil lamps at night or window light by day. Of course, those windows are no help these days; they were painted black during the Second World War, when this place was used as a barracks and a hospital. I guess no one ever saw fit to strip the paint off the windows.

I turn the peppermint over in my mouth as I scrape the tuna fish into Jinx's bowl. I'll listen to Isabelle for a few minutes, then go do my chores.

"Hello."

I scream and drop the container.

"You!" I say, trying to regain myself, which is hard to do after shrieking in front of someone.

"I'm Tara," she says. She tips her head and waits.

Tara. It's the sound of wind and branches blowing, dark and mysterious.

"Sorry," she says, except it comes out as *sore-y.* "I didn't mean to scare you. Are you all right then?"

"I'm all right." Usually this room is invitation-only, but immediately I make an exception for her. I want to know why she was hiding, why she swam in her clothes, why she's wearing that same outfit, and where the heck she's been all this time. "I'm Allie Jo."

She smiles. "I know."

I sure do like her accent. "Where you from?"

Something changes in her eyes when I ask that, like a transparent shade coming down. I can still see her, but it's like I can't see in.

"Around, all over. I'm from a lot of places."

"Military." I nod my head. Military kids move all the time. No wonder she has an accent. In school, there's a kid from an Air Force family who was born in England and has an English accent. When he turns eighteen, he gets to choose which country he'll be a citizen of.

I study Tara carefully. "Are you eighteen yet?" I wonder which country she'll choose.

"I'm sixteen." She pulls her hair forward and strokes it.

Luminous. That's the word I think of. I heard it on a shampoo commercial. Her hair is luminous; it shimmers in the light. She looks like a mermaid.

"You're so pretty." I slap my hand to my mouth. I can't believe I just said that out loud.

She laughs, but not in an I'm-making-fun-of-you way. It's a gentle laugh, a nice laugh, not snippy, which is how Jennifer Jorgensen would laugh. And this girl is way prettier than Jennifer—she's beautiful.

"You're pretty too," she says, and smiles.

My face heats up a little. Well, where are my manners? "Whyn't you sit down?" I sit on the carpet remnant, leaving the beanbag for her. But she sits on the carpet across from me, folding her legs like a dancer. Her posture is straight; without even thinking, I pull myself up out of my slouch.

Rain patters lightly outside, filtering through the jacaranda leaves; orchid petals float down with the raindrops.

Tara gasps. "The creature!"

"What?" I snap my head around. "That's Jinx!" Jinx leaps down from the window and sidles up against me. I rub her back. She's a little damp from the rain.

She slips out from under my hand and pushes her side into Tara's leg. Tara laughs and pets Jinx. "Her fur is soft."

It makes me feel good that she likes my cat and my cat

likes her. Sophie did nothing but sneeze when I brought her up here, but it's not her fault she's allergic.

"I thought I saw you at breakfast the other day," I say, "but it wasn't you. Where've you been?"

She laughs, and it floats around me like dandelions—soft and breezy. "I wanted to see you," she says. Though her eyes are black, they glitter with light.

I look up at her. "You did?"

"Yes. Just as you wanted to see me."

I stop for a minute. She's right. I *did* want to see her. "Wow . . ."

The sky outside darkens. A gust blows in and rustles the kudzu, causing a monarch to close its wings and hold on tight.

She tilts her head and watches me closely as she asks, "Did you keep our secret?" It's a question, but she says it like a sentence. "Did you tell anyone about me?"

I nod. "I mean"—I shake my head—"I didn't tell anyone about you."

Thunder rumbles gently from far away.

She watches as Jinx pads up to the tuna and starts chowing down. I watch her watch Jinx; she licks her lips and swallows.

Turning to me, she says, "I'm hungry. The black shells have no meat in them, but the fish is delicious." She steals a glance at Jinx and licks her lips again.

THE SUMMER OF MOONLIGHT SECRETS

"Tuna salad," I say. No wonder I never see her. She must hit the lunch buffet; I always eat lunch at home. "I don't think Chef has turned over the menu yet, but we could go down and get breakfast."

She shakes her head. "Too many people."

"There aren't too many people!" That won't happen till Taste of Hope, when the hotel bulges with people staying over for the festival.

"Allie Jo," she says, laying her hand on me. Her hair grazes my arm and a shiver goes right down to my feet. She holds me still with her gaze. "You're my friend; I picked you. I feel strength and goodness in you."

"You do?" I like strength and goodness. "Do you feel anything else in me?" If she does, I want to know—maybe it's something really cool, like I discover a new planet or win the lottery. "Are you a gypsy?"

She throws her head back and laughs. "You ask a lot of questions." Then her smile fades and she straightens up. Her eyes pierce mine deeply. "I'm just a girl, like you."

Jinx leaves her bowl and climbs onto the beanbag. Spreading out her paws, she kneads it like dough, then curls up and settles into it. I become aware that the rain has stopped; plus, Dad'll be expecting me for the brass. Polishing brass is one job I never miss because I actually get paid for it.

"I have to go," I say, standing. She stands up too. "You don't have to leave," I quickly offer. I'd kind of like to think of her here, enjoying the place. A warm breeze swirls into the room, gently touching the leaves. The bark on the jacaranda branches has darkened from the rain, causing the light green of the leaves to stand out. "Why don't you stay?"

"I would like that," she says. "Allie Jo?" she calls as I head out the doorway. "Don't tell anyone I'm here—do you promise?"

"You won't get in trouble. I won't tell your parents." Isabelle didn't tell her parents that Karen flunked a math test because Karen and her best friend were too busy passing notes in class to pay attention.

"But do you promise?"

I nod. I don't do anything silly like *pinky promise* or *cross my heart and hope to die*. Her face is so serious I get the feeling the promise is about more than just her being on prohibited grounds. In fact, I'm sure of it.

18

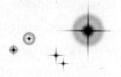

When Tara neared Allie Jo, sensations flooded her—kindness, strength, loyalty, and another one, a kind of loneliness. Why did humans suffer so? She'd felt similar vibrations from the one she later learned was called Chase, except his vibes leaped through her system like electrical charges. Wave upon wave crashed within her—his fierce loyalty, boldness, and wisdom, and under it, intense currents of sadness, loneliness.

She'd begun to feel these things too. She tried to close her ears, shut these sensations out, but it didn't work. How did they live with this noise in their souls? At times, she thought she might not bear it, that she might crumble under the weight of it.

She sat in this room, lush with green plants and other living things. The jinx slept. She reached over to the bowl and finished off the tuna.

The old ones warned them of others who had never returned. She and her friends listened with big, brown eyes, but after the elders slipped away, she and her friends giggled at the stories, throwing their heads back until every word of warning floated away on bubbles of laughter.

Would now that she'd heeded the words of the old ones.

19

Chase

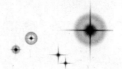

No one ever tells you how much it rains in Florida. It should be called the Rain State, not the Sunshine State.

Stuck inside again. As I pass the front desk, Clay stops me.

"Message from your dad," he says, handing me a pink paper that says, *I'm at a truck stop near Gainesville. I-75 is jammed up from some accident. Not sure how late I'll be.*

I sigh.

"Tough luck, right?" Clay leans forward on the desk. "Why's your dad always gone?"

"He's a writer. He's got this big travel assignment down here and I was supposed to do everything with him, but—" I lift my cast up.

"Bummer," he says.

"Tell me about it."

He pushes up from the desk. "Well, have a good one."

"Thanks." I watch as he walks back into the office. I feel like dinging him back over here just for someone to talk to.

I wander out into the empty hallway. Lightning flashes, so at first I think I'm seeing an optical illusion, but no, it's true—a wall panel creaks open. Cool! Very cool. I don't remember *that* being mentioned on the tour.

I sprint down the hall. "Whoa! Allie Jo!"

She startles big-time.

I check out the wall behind her. No door handle, no hinges that I can see. "How did you get in there?" I ask, running my hands along the wall. "Is that a secret room? Open it up!"

She acts like she didn't hear me, starts walking toward the front desk.

"Allie Jo!" I say. When I see she's not stopping for me, I run ahead of her and jog backward. "Where you going? You *have* to show me that hidden panel—that's so cool!"

"What're you talking about?" she asks without stopping.

Clay's back at the front desk and Allie Jo walks around and comes up with a bottle and some rags.

"That panel," I say. I turn to Clay. "She just came out of a secret panel."

He cocks an eyebrow at her.

Opening the bottle, she pours some cleaner on the rag and swipes the brass rail. "Move, please."

I lift my hand before she polishes it. "Is there a secret panel down there?" I glance from her to Clay.

He raises his palms and chuckles. "I'm not saying anything."

"Okay," I say, straightening up. "I'll go find out for myself." I march away from the desk.

"Get back here!" Allie Jo orders.

A grin crosses my face, but I wipe it off before I turn around.

"Ye-es?" I ask.

She glances around, furrows her eyebrows, and motions for me to come closer. Taking my time, I swing my arm and whistle. But I can't wait to hear the secret. I lean on the rail.

She looks at me and drops her shoulders. "First of all," she says, "you just messed up my work."

"Oh!" I pop my hand off. Sure enough, my fingerprints stand out on the brass.

"Second of all, only employees are allowed to know this stuff, so . . ." She runs her eyes over my cast. "How good are you at polishing brass?"

"Do I get paid?"

She huffs at me.

I try to cross my arms, but it doesn't work so well with the cast. "Employees *always* get paid."

She gives me a hard look. "There's almost a quarter-mile of brass on this floor. You think you're up to it?"

I scoff at her. "Gimme those rags."

She pushes a clean rag into my hand. "Employees are usually on a three-week probation," she says, pursing her lips. "But I'll let you get by on three days."

"Three days!"

She shrugs.

"Just show me what to do," I say. I don't mind making some money. Besides, I intend to figure out those panels before three days are up.

20

Allie Jo

Even though it's daytime, the porch behind Dad's office is shady enough to invite mosquitoes, and they're needling the heck out of me. I swat one on my shin and my own blood smears on my leg. *Blech.* I flick the mosquito off and wipe my hand on my shorts.

Sophie's fingers fly over her knitting needles; if she goes any faster, smoke will come off them.

"Have you seen Chase today?" she asks, eyes on her knitting.

I push the glider back and we sway under the fan. "He went somewhere with his dad." Then I tell her about him working for me yesterday and how he is now an employee but still has two days left of probation.

She steals a glance at me. "What do you think of him?"

"Well, he's a pretty good worker, and he'd be even better with two arms, but—" I look at her face. "*Oh!*" I say. "You mean, what do I *think* of him, right?"

She bites her lip and grins.

A smile plays on my mouth. "Okay . . ." I wonder if I should tell her that I think he likes her too, which I'm almost positive he does, but since I haven't discussed it with him, it's sort of a secret. "Yeah, he's pretty cool."

"And cute!" she bursts out. We both laugh for a moment before getting lost in thought.

One thing I love about this porch is that the jacaranda tree has decorated the ground with orchid petals. Dark green azalea bushes encircle the trunk, but they already bloomed in spring; now they're setting their buds for next year.

"*Eew!*" Sophie snatches her feet up onto the swing.

I inspect the floorboards. "Just a lizard. They don't bite." He starts his lizard push-ups.

"What's he doing?"

She seems so grossed out. It makes me think of Melanie and her trick and I laugh out loud. "He's showing off, like this is his territory."

I slam one foot onto the floor and he scurries away. They're especially gross if you accidentally snap off their tail and the tail just wiggles on its own while the lizard escapes. I'm careful not to catch the tail under my heel.

"Yuck," Sophie says, then leans over and inspects my scarf. "Good job."

"Thanks." I glance over at hers, which is a good foot longer than mine. "I've just been kind of busy." *With Tara.* Suddenly, I'm aching to tell her about Tara, how pretty she is and how wise she seems. But I know how to keep a secret. Instead, I say, "We're getting ready for Taste of Hope."

She takes on a look of recognition. "Oh! You mean that big festival on July Fourth?"

"Yeah!" I'm pleased she knows about it.

"I can't wait to go! It sounds like fun!"

She knits without looking. I watch as a whole row comes out of nowhere.

"You know," I say, considering her speed, "I've got to help assemble favors for The Meriwether." I get a big boost in my allowance because there's so much work to do. Usually, Dad lets me pay the boys to help, but having people around my age to help with the work is even better. So I say very casually, "I could use another employee."

She stops knitting. "You mean me? I would get paid?"

Enthusiasm is a quality I like in my employees. "You could help me hand them out at Taste of Hope too."

All the restaurants and boutiques around here have booths where they give stuff away. It's fun because The Meriwether puts up a booth and I get to pass out free samples of our food. We also have brochures, but I like passing out the food better because when you hand someone a flyer, they don't really care, but when you hand them some food, they are always happy.

Sophie's whole face lights up. "That sounds like fun!"

"It is!" I tell her how we'll get to wear waitress uniforms and have our hair all fancy, and we'll still get to go around and get stuff from the other booths. "People come from all over the country for this," I say. "Everyone turns out."

"I wonder if Chase will go," she says.

I'm glad I don't like a boy. It seems to control all your thoughts.

The glider sways back and forth. Absentmindedly, I say, "I wonder where his mom is."

"What do you mean?"

"I mean, first he told me she was visiting other people; then he told me she was gone, like *disappeared* or something."

Sophie stops knitting. "Disappeared? Like, what do you mean?"

I shrug. "I don't know. He sort of got mad at me when I tried to ask him." It can't be good, though. And it sinks in now that maybe *this* was a secret. Me and my big mouth.

21

Chase

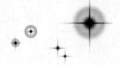

I'm encrusted with salt and I smell like a fish, but I am happy.

Today Dad and I drove to St. Pete to explore the area and ride in something called a Duck. It's this bus that takes you on a tour of the city. The driver talks about the history of the area, and then all of a sudden the bus splashes into the water and you're sailing!

By now, the sun was setting and Dad was gazing off into the distance, looking all writerly. I could practically read his thoughts: *The breeze washed the man and his son in the scent of the bay. Coloring the sky in hues of orange and watermelon red, the sun melted into the horizon, leaving the father and his boy in awe at such glory.* Dad had his head in his camera bag when I saw a black fin circle out of the water behind the boat.

Shark!

"Folks, if you look behind us, you'll see we've got some dolphin friends."

Okay, dolphins! The crowd gasped, and lucky for me and Dad, we were sitting in the last row. Two dolphins launched out of the water and nose-dived back in. Everyone broke into applause. Then they loop-de-looped across the surface—real dolphins! *Click, whir; click, whir*—the sound of Dad's camera, capturing it all.

My skin is sticky and so is my hair.

"You first in the shower," Dad says once we're back in our room. He slips his bag off his shoulder and starts going through it. I tease him about carrying a purse, but it's really more of a soft briefcase he keeps all his notebooks and stuff in. "Hey, where—" He scans the tabletop. "I left a notebook in the car. Be right back."

Right after he leaves, the phone rings.

It's Gail, one of the ladies Dad works with. I picture her permed brown hair and painted nails.

"Hey, hon. How ya doing?" she asks.

"Broke my arm," I say.

"Oh, no! That kind of puts a damper on your vacation."

"Tell me about it." Gail's cool. Too bad she's got a crush on Dad.

"Your dad there? I've got to get some expenses from him." Ah, using work as the excuse to call.

"He's out—"

She gasps. "He's out?"

"He's getting something from the car. He'll be right in."

"Oh," she says. I bet she doesn't know how relieved her voice sounds.

We do the small-talk thing until Dad walks in.

"Hi, Gail. Let me get my papers," he says when I hand him the phone. Nothing like whispering sweet nothings into someone's ear.

Poor Gail and her curly hair. Dad is still in love with Mom.

22

Allie Jo

The gazebo is lit up with white Christmas lights, the little kind. They hang from the gingerbread trim like crystals, making the whole thing look like an old-fashioned jewelry box. A couple of old oaks hang low near the gazebo, the lace of Spanish moss touching the roof. Opening one of the French doors of the Emerald Dining Room, I step onto the veranda and head out to the gazebo.

After we'd cleared the supper dishes, Mom started washing and Dad got a towel to dry. I swear, two lovebirds.

"Can I go sit on the Emerald veranda?" I asked. Summer nights are especially nice, with the moon shining down on the springs. Sometimes I sit in the gazebo and listen to crickets.

"Go ahead, honey," Mom said. "Just come back in before too long."

The lemony smell of the citronella lamps drifts in the air. I like that smell. I like the way the fire flickers in the lamps, which look like streetlamps from the old days. Dad ordered them a few years ago to keep down the mosquitoes. Good thing, too, because I hate to spend my evening swatting at bugs.

I turn off the gazebo lights, sit on the bench, and gaze out over the springs. Stars twinkle, and if you could hear them, I bet they'd sound like the crickets, who chirp in the dusk. Frogs join in with their rubber-band melody.

Leaning back against the post, I stretch my legs out along the bench and let out a deep breath. This is just the kind of summer night I love. I sit back and let the chirping and the twanging fill my ears.

This morning when I turned on the tape recorder, Isabelle said her favorite ride at Disney World was the Grand Prix Raceway because her mom let her lean over and steer the car. *So I know how to drive now,* she said. *Why didn't you go on it?*

Karen's voice came from a little ways off. Television noises played in the background. *'Cause I went on Space Mountain with Dad. Besides, I have my license now, so I can drive* real *cars.*

Isabelle got very close to the microphone and said, *Karen is sixteen. She's a good driver.*

It must be nice having an older sister.

I shift on the gazebo bench, rambling over my day, and then I notice it—the melodies have cranked up in volume. It's like they have loudspeakers. Sitting up, I look around.

The full moon casts a yellow light on the grounds, moonbeams skipping over ripples in the spring. I get to my feet. The springwater surges, almost lapping over the concrete pad. The springhead bubbles wildly, noisily, louder and louder.

My heart whirls in my chest. The spring is going to explode! *Run! Run!* I tell myself, but I'm rooted to the spot.

Huge fish jump out and splash down, one after the other; then, across the darkness on the concrete, I can just make out small, leaping shapes. The frogs! They're jumping, making their way around the pad as if they're following something.

Then I see it, the thing they're following, a big thing. It bobs up for a second, but in the moonlight, I only make out the dark shimmer of its head.

I gasp loudly.

Everything stops. The frogs scuttle into the grass, the fish glide underwater, and the springs settle down to a gentle murmur. Within seconds, the crickets begin their chirping, joined by the frogs and their deep voices.

I can't believe what I've seen. I pore over the water, which is now calm except for the gentle boil from the springhead. I stare, trying to figure out what just happened.

Then a moonbeam hits a glistening shape emerging from the water. My eyes hollow out. My heart hammers against my ribs. I scream, but all that comes out is a horrible rasp. Long, black tendrils, water rolling right off them—it's some kind of creature! My feet run, but all I'm doing is jogging in place.

"Allie Jo," the shape says, then parts its hair. "Don't be scared—it's only me."

My mouth drops open. My heart still hammers, but it slows as she approaches and I see it's her. It's really her—*Tara*.

23

Chase

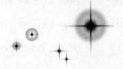

I stare at the full moon from our hotel room.

"Close those blinds, will you, Chase?" Fresh out of his shower, Dad rummages through the hotel dresser for clean clothes.

When I was little and we drove places, I thought the moon followed us; it was always there, no matter which way Dad turned the car. I didn't know how that was possible.

Then, when he started traveling, he'd call us at night, Aunt Sheila and me. When it was my turn to talk, he told me to look out the window. *Are you looking at the moon?* he'd ask. I'd nod, cupping the phone. *I am too*, he'd say. That seemed like magic, like it was connecting us.

I wonder if Mom is looking at it.

But that's just a silly kid thing. I snap the blinds shut and plop onto my bed. "What do you want to do?"

"Nothing." He pulls exercise shorts over his boxers. "I'm pretty wiped out." He stretches out on his bed, aims the remote. "Let's see what's on TV."

My shoulders sink. I pace from the windows across to the door, stopping to read the evacuation plan. Got it. Don't use the elevators. Use the stairs. I march back to the windows, back to the door, back to the windows, back to the—

"Chase!"

I freeze with my arms in midswing.

He motions with his hand for me to move. "I can't see the TV with you walking back and forth like that."

"I thought when we came back we were going to do something."

He sighs, hits the Mute button. "Sorry, bud. I can hardly lift this remote."

Dropping my arms, I let my whole body sag. "Come on, Dad. At least go with me to the game room."

Dad points to the dresser with his remote. "My wallet's right there."

Three fives and a one. He's buying me off, and I accept the offer. Anything's better than staying in here and just watching TV.

Once downstairs, I'm not thinking Pac-Man; I'm

thinking ice cream, but the girl is already mopping the floor of the ice-cream parlor. "Try the dining room," she says. "I think they're still open."

The hallway is dark during the day, but at night it's downright creepy, the perfect setting for a mystery: *Shadows pressed against the walls, holding their secrets close. Who had walked these halls before? The boy strained to see, but the cobwebbed lamps allowed little illumination. The boy hastened his errand.*

I swipe a peppermint from the front of the dining room. I don't see a hostess, so I walk in. I kind of like having the place to myself. Unwrapping my peppermint, I sit down at a table in the middle. Too hard. I leave the plastic wrapper on the table and move on. Hmm, this one is too soft. I weave my way around and take a seat by the windows. Ah, just right. I put my feet up on the chair across from me and stare out the window.

"Um, the kitchen's closed." The guy appears out of nowhere.

My feet jerk to the floor. "Do I have to leave?"

The guy shrugs. "Sorry, dude. We've got to vacuum and change out table tents . . ."

He's waiting for me to get up.

I sigh and push my chair back, then spot the French doors. I bet I could see the moon really well from the dock. "Can I go out there?"

He glances over his shoulder, then back to me. "I'm about to lock those doors," he says. "But just come back in by the pool."

Cool. I swing a French door open and a gust of wind pushes me. I hear a dead bolt fall into place behind me, followed by a top lock and a slider. Geez, who do they think's coming in?

A huge porch wraps around the dining room, but it's got an overhang, and I won't be able to see the moon or the stars. I move off the porch, down the steps, and into the darkness; it's the best way to see the light.

Yep, Big Dipper, Little Dipper, bunch of other stars I don't know the names of.

I stare at the full moon. Man in the moon. Green cheese moon. Turn-me-into-a-werewolf moon. That would be cool.

Full moon.

It hits me—I don't know—like a pain in my chest. I told Dad about this once before; he said it was growing pains. But I kept complaining about it, so the doctor had me X-rayed, said I had a good heart, and sent me to a counselor, who said I had a sad heart and needed to talk about it.

I didn't want to talk to the counselor, but he was eager to fix me. Finally, just to satisfy him and get the sessions over with, I told him I missed my mother, that I felt her in my bones, that I had some sense of her even though I was only, like, two when she left.

After a while, he proclaimed me *cured*.

I stare at the moon. Man, something hurts. I head back in to Dad.

24

Allie Jo

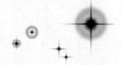

I am squished so low in the gazebo I think my knees are going to bust. What is so interesting about that moon? It feels like Chase has been staring at it for hours. I can just make him out through the lattice.

Oh, my gosh, I need to pull my legs out, but I don't dare because he might hear me. Streaks of pain race along my neck from tilting my head at a weird angle, but I hold this position. I am aware of everything—my heartbeat, my breathing, the crickets, the frogs. I feel like I did when I drank Mom's coffee once; every single nerve throbs with energy. It's kind of exciting.

Go, go, go! I can't be crimped down like this for much longer. A caterpillar climbs onto my flip-flop and crawls over my toes. It tickles, but I don't dare move.

Tara taps my shoulder and I almost yelp. Craning my

head around, I glance at her and she gestures toward the pool, where Chase is slipping through the hotel door, back inside.

I bolt upright and shake my foot. The caterpillar goes flying. That's practice for when he becomes a butterfly later.

"Whew!" I laugh and turn to Tara. "He didn't see us! That was great." It was her idea to hide from him.

She peers over the lawn, then gets up and sits on the bench, sopping wet. She's wearing the same clothes she had on yesterday. I guess her mom didn't pack a lot of outfits.

Even though it's muggy outside, the springs are seventy-two degrees all year round. I touch her arm. "You must be freezing!" I say.

She seems to think about this as she rubs water droplets off her arms. "I'm not used to swimming without my coat."

"Your coat?"

Her eyes widen for second. "I mean . . ." She laughs. "Perhaps I *am* cold!" Leaning her head, she drapes her hair to her side and twists it, wringing out the water. "And wet!"

"I'll get you a towel!" I dash over to the cabinet and come back with a nice, fluffy towel.

She wraps it around herself like a cape. Even sopping wet, she could be a model—she's that pretty. She dabs her face with the towel, then lowers her arm.

"I like it here," she says.

"Me too," I reply. "The gazebo and the garden room are tied for my favorite spots."

"I mean, I like everything here." Turning to me, she asks, "Have you enjoyed growing up in this place?"

"Oh, yeah!" The Meriwether is like my own little town, and I know all the villagers—Clay, Chef, the cooks, the housekeepers. My dad is like the mayor and my mom is the first lady. And don't forget the privileges. "From my bedroom to the counter at The Meriwether's ice cream parlor are two hundred and fifty-three steps." I know this because I've had more than one occasion to count them. "I get blueberry pancakes every morning and everyone here knows me." I give her some tidbits from the tour, not the whole spiel, of course, but just the stuff about the old days. "I love living here," I say.

She takes it all in, everything I've just described. "It's quite beautiful," she says.

A warmth pours over me and settles into my heart. The Meriwether is part of me; it's built into my bones. Hearing how she feels about it makes me like her even more.

As she pulls the towel off her shoulders, I can't get over how graceful she is. And soaked. "Do you want to go in? You should probably change into something dry."

I stand up, thinking she's going to do the same, but she only watches me. I quickly sit back down again. "Um ... ."

The look she gives me is direct and open. I don't know why, but it scares me a little.

"I don't have anything dry," she says.

I know she's waiting for me to say something, but her words don't make sense. My head tilts.

"I have no other clothes."

I pull my head back and laugh a little, like I do when I'm nervous. "What?" Is she playing a joke on me? But when I look at her hard, I see she's dead serious. "But you're on vacation!"

Slowly, she shakes her head while staring directly at me. "I'm not on vacation, Allie Jo." Her eyes gleam in the darkness.

"I ran away."

25

Chase

It was blazing hot when we first got out here. My skin fried under the heat and sweat trickled from my cast. The only relief was the thin clouds that blocked the sun for a few minutes; now clouds fill the whole sky. Still, it's one of the best days so far—Sophie sits next to me, splashing her feet in the ice-cold water.

Looking at her makes me nervous. I stare into the water instead. Clouds in the sky are reflected in the water below.

"Man, this is cold," I say. "I can't feel my feet any-more." But I'm still hot.

Sophie laughs. "I'm freezing."

I steal a quick glance at her and see goose bumps on her arms. It's funny how you can be cold and hot at the same time.

A tall, grayish bird flies over the spring and settles in the cattails. He walks like a flamingo.

"Are you and your dad having a good vacation?" Sophie asks. She draws her feet up from the water and shivers. I picture myself wrapping my arms around her just to keep her warm.

Every night, Dad hunches over his typewriter, his notes strewn all over the desk. But then again, he *has* to work. He brought me here with him, and right now, at this very moment, I wouldn't want to be anywhere else. "Definitely," I say, staring straight at her because I can't help it. "Definitely a good vacation."

She smiles, bites her lip, and bends her head for a second. When she looks up, she goes, "I'm having a good vacation too."

I feel that current again, like when two magnets pull to each other. My eyes sweep down her face, over her shoulders and arms, which are still covered with goose bumps. Without even thinking, I reach back and pull my shirt off, fumbling to get it over the cast.

Sophie's mouth is an *O*.

I hand the shirt to her. "Put it on," I say. "You'll warm up." I act nonchalant, but I feel good, like a guy who just threw his coat over a puddle so a lady could walk across.

She pulls the shirt on and it drops loosely over her

head. Scooping her knees into it, she says, "Thanks." A little smile crosses her lips and she looks down.

I look away. The sight of her with my shirt on makes me feel like a lion. My chest fills with pride. My heart turns to mush. I've never had this feeling before.

I steal a glance at her and she looks my way at the same time and we laugh.

Wisps of hair cover her eyes. I want so badly to reach over and smooth them away.

"Who's your mom visiting?" she asks.

Something near my heart strikes up. "What?"

Sophie puts her hand near mine. "I heard she was visiting some other people." Her voice is tender. "Is she coming back?"

I peer over the edge at my reflection wavering in the water. I see my face, which has Mom's eyes and cheekbones, and I see the springs right through myself, depending on how I focus. Moss-covered pebbles line the bottom; it's only a few feet deep right here.

Why not? I think. I jump in feetfirst, making sure to hold my broken parts up.

Sophie screams and shrinks back from the spray. "Aren't you freezing?" she asks, laughing.

Freezing? I'm totally numb. I laugh and pretend to splash her. "It's just right," I say. "I can't feel a thing."

26

Allie Jo

Tara is a runaway!

If only Dad hadn't come onto the veranda looking for me. I couldn't sleep at all last night thinking about Tara. Why was she running away? I concocted all sorts of stories about her, but only one made sense: she had a cruel step-mother.

This would explain why she had no bathing suit and no extra clothes. The stepmother wouldn't buy her any, of course; she bought stuff only for her own daughters. I simmered in my bed, thinking about poor Tara, doing all the work and being treated like a servant. No wonder she ran away.

I gobbled down my pancakes this morning and made lots of noise during my inspections, but Tara didn't show up. I daydreamed through all my chores, through my baby-sitting job, and all the way through supper.

I ate everything on my plate, including the onions, and cleared the table. "I'm going to sit on the veranda," I call out.

Dad flicked me with a dish towel. "Don't stay out so late tonight, okay?"

But it's not Tara I find outside; it's Chase. He's sitting on the concrete pad, his feet stirring in the water. I did the brass by myself today, since he was with his dad.

"Hi," I say.

He startles, or at least it seems like he does. "Hey," he says.

A lizard scurries away from me. "What are you doing?"

"Looking at the moon. It was full yesterday."

I gaze up and see that the moon is a fingernail short of being full.

"Did you ever see *Teen Wolf*?" he asks.

I shake my head. "I don't like scary movies."

"It's not scary! It's about this guy who plays basketball and becomes a werewolf."

I pinch up my face. "Knock, knock," I say, dropping beside him.

He plays along. "Who's there?"

"Werewolf."

"Werewolf who?"

"Shut up and comb your face."

He groans. "Har, har."

I plunk my feet into the water. It sends a chill right up my spine.

Chase notices my shiver and laughs. "My dad says that people in Florida have thin blood. That's why you get cold so easily."

I've heard that too. "I wonder if that's true."

He shrugs his shoulders and lies back on the dock. Crickets and frogs bleat in harmony. Chase raises his left arm. "Big Dipper."

I point. "Little Dipper." I lie down.

"Moon."

"That's not a star!"

"I know," he says. We stare at the night sky for a minute. Then he goes, "I asked your mom about that secret panel."

I'm not worried. Mom doesn't like guests going in there, something about insurance. It'll be different after Chase has passed his probation. "What'd she say?"

"She said it went up to the nanny quarters?"

I take a deep breath and make my eyes huge when I look at him. "Didn't she tell you?"

"Tell me what?" He bolts upright.

I sit up too. "I don't know if I should be telling you this."

"Oh, man! You have to!" He gawks at me.

I look around and hunch down. All I need is a flash-light to hold up under my chin. "The staircase goes up to the nanny quarters—that's where the nannies stayed with all the rich people's kids. There was one nanny, sixteen; she was an indentured servant from Ireland and her master liked her better than his wife." That part's true, according to legend. Now for the part I like best, the part I made up. I lean in close and say in a hoarse voice, "The wife bricked her in while she slept."

"No!" Chase says. His whole face lights up.

"Yes!" I say. "And sometimes, late at night, you can hear her clawing to get out."

"No way!" But he wants to believe; he halfway believes—I can tell.

He lies back down with a smile on his face. The arm with the cast on it lies across his stomach. It reminds me that his mom won't be able to sign it; it reminds me of something else too.

"Um," I say, "I sort of accidentally told Sophie about your mom."

He turns his head on the ground to look at me. "What'd you say?"

"That she was gone." I don't want to admit that I said *disappeared* too. Anyway, she has to come back; she's his *mother*.

Chase pushes himself up and slumps, his feet still in the water. "If I tell you something, you can't tell anyone."

I swallow and raise my eyebrows. "I won't tell anyone."

"My mom ran away." He stares at me, waiting for a response.

"What?"

"When I was really little, my mom took off." His voice cracks. "She left us."

My heart drops to my stomach when he says that. It's not so much his words as it is hearing his voice crack. I wish I could put a cast on his heart.

27

Chase

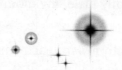

In two weeks, I'll get my short cast. I still won't be able to go swimming, but it sure will be easier to zip up my pants. A real plus, I think, as I struggle into my shorts before heading out. I'm looking for Allie Jo on day three of my probation, but I can't find her anywhere.

"Try the sunporch," Mr. Jackson says when I stop by the front desk.

Ever since I told Allie Jo about my mom, I feel better, like I'm not carrying this big, dark secret around. I used to lie to people, tell them my mom was dead or that my parents were divorced, but then they'd ask too many questions and I'd forget which story I told to which person, and keeping up with it all got really complicated. Sometimes it's easier to stick with the truth. Or say nothing.

Heading down to the sunporch, I realize no one else is

in the hallway. I lean out. Nope, no one can see me from the front desk or the dining room. I start pressing the wall like crazy. Where's that secret panel? I push and I pound and then I hear a hollow sound.

After fumbling around for a minute, I press on this wooden trim piece and, easy as that, the panel opens. I jump in and it closes behind me, clicking shut. Suddenly, it's dark, and I realize why—the only window I can see has been painted black. The wind howls outside and rain beats against the wall. High above, the staircase groans. My heart beats a little faster. As my eyes adjust, I make out a string hanging over a landing before the stairs turn. I can make it that far before anything grabs me.

The stairs are bare wood and open, like bleachers. I hate walking on bleachers; I always feel like I'll fall right through the gaps. Gripping the wooden handrail, I plant my foot on the first step. It cracks. I suck air in and freeze. Nothing. No one's heard me. I don't know if that's good or bad.

I reach the landing and pull the string. The bulb casts a weak, yellowish light over the rest of the stairs, which turn up from the landing alongside a rough, crumbling wall—a dungeon wall. When I lean my hand against it, I feel moisture. The rotting smell of mildew hangs in the air.

The steps twist into the darkness before the next landing. I wave my hand around, trying to feel for the string, but I stumble back against the wall and hit a post. A long skeleton finger uncurls and hooks my shirt on its bony tip. It tries to pull me back to the corner. I scream, jerk away, and scramble up a couple of flights as something clatters to the ground.

Huffing and puffing, I crouch, clutching the banister. Spiderwebs stick to my fingers, but I don't care. Then I hear something above the wind, something above the rain, something like . . . something like *clawing*. The bricked-in nanny! Then a door softly shuts—I can't tell where; my heart's beating too loudly. The wind is roaring, and she's up there, scratching the bricks with her fingers.

I fly down the stairs, barely registering the old-fashioned window hook as I pass the landing. As I swing around the banister, a dark shape emerges. I shriek and stiffen as if hit by an electrical shock.

Grasping the rail for balance, my eyes light on the figure in front of me. I sag against the banister, gasping for air. My heart's banging like crazy in my chest, but it's beginning to settle.

Lifting my gaze to the specter again, I break into laughter. It's not a zombie nanny or a raggedy old ghost.

"It's you!"

28

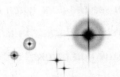

Fear spiraled in the boy's wake. As the current pushed down toward her, Tara waited for him to appear.

"It's you!" he shouted upon seeing her.

Waves from his flight down the stairs crashed over her. She knew there was nothing to fear, not here, not in this hotel. She'd explored its halls, trailing her fingertips along the walls. Whispers came to her, but she could not hear them clearly. Voices from too long ago. Stronger were the trails left by Allie Jo. The girl's presence was everywhere.

"Yes," she said. "It's me."

Rushes of air curled around him, settling at his feet like dust.

"Come," she said. Without glancing back, she ascended the stairs. She knew he would follow.

Pushing open a scuffed door with a hand-painted 3 on it, she led him onto the third floor.

"Cool!" the boy said after the panel shut behind them. "Look! You can't even see the door when it's closed."

She smiled to herself. He lacked much in vision.

"This is where I saw you before," the boy said. "You know, where I broke my arm." He gestured wildly as he spoke; energy rolled off him in sparks. "Thanks for helping me, by the way."

Looking up, he asked, "What's your name?"

"What's *your* name?" she quickly asked.

"Chase." He fell silent for a moment. "Where are we going?"

They'd gone far down the hall, almost to the end. A light path ran the length of the hall where carpet once lay. Circular scrapes marred the heart-of-pine flooring. Shadows of beauty crossed in the air but were lost in the true vision: dead roaches lying on their backs; paint peeling, hanging from the walls like ribbons. Some walls had been hacked, exposing the heartwood that supported the hotel.

She bent down and ran her fingers over a deep gouge.

His eyes widened with recognition. "That's what tripped me up! I fell there"—he glanced at her—"right?"

Tara nodded.

She stood, and he rose, looking up at her like a pup.

"So what are you doing?" He jumped around her. "You want to explore this place? It's got all kinds of secret rooms."

Stiffening, she remembered the secret room the man had

locked her in. There had been no windows, but she could see well in the dark. No, it wasn't the darkness that had bothered her; it was his plans that scared her—plans he spoke of with great excitement and agitation. When two days had passed, she heard him leave, and she splintered the door open with one powerful kick.

The boy before her now was speaking of secret rooms. She tipped her head and observed him. "What is it you seek?"

"'Seek?'" The boy laughed. "You kind of have an accent. Where are you from?"

Words—she must be more careful with them. It was best not to use too many, she realized, at least until she learned to speak as they did. But she liked him; she felt a kindred spirit in him.

"Irish," she said. "Scottish." She remembered the waves of the deep, surging and cresting, the joy she felt in their power.

The boy smiled. "I'm part Irish too!"

Black Irish, she thought. Dark hair and blue eyes. She had chosen right in this boy. His aura was good.

A breeze fluttered through her hair, lifting the ends. The other one was coming. She waited expectantly.

29

Allie Jo

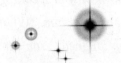

I almost have a heart attack when I spot two people huddled down the hall of the third floor. "Hey!" I yell. Clenching my fists, I march toward them, ready to give them H-E-you-know-what for being up here, so it feels like a punch in the gut when I get closer and see it's Tara—*with Chase.*

My mouth drops. I look from Chase to Tara and back to Chase. "Hey, what are you doing?" I try to act casual; I thought she was just *my* secret.

He gestures toward Tara. "She just—" He looks at her. "What's your name?"

There's a moment, just a fraction of a second, in which she seems to measure him up. Then she says, "Tara."

I breathe in shallow puffs. She told me not to tell anyone and now here she is telling Chase everything.

"Don't be mad, Allie Jo," Tara says, her voice smoothing

me over the way I smooth Jinx's fur. "You are both my friends."

"You guys know each other?" Chase asks, his head tilting. He looks at Tara. "Where've you been? I haven't seen you since I broke my arm."

My eyebrows flash up. "*You* guys know each other?"

Tara's laughter sprinkles over us. "*You* guys know each other too?"

Chase laughs, watching Tara with wide-open admiration. He's barely looked away from her since I got here.

I'm about to sit down when Tara shakes her head.

Standing, she says, "I must go. Too long in one place."

It's been days since I've seen her. "I'm going with you," I say.

"Me too," says Chase, getting up on his feet. As we follow behind Tara, Chase looks at me. "Tara and I are both Irish," he says, as if it's some exclusive club that only they are the members of.

"Tara and I go swimming at night," I counter, even though, officially, I didn't swim.

Chase grins. "Cool! Next time, get me."

I look sideways at Chase. "You can't," I say, pointing to his cast.

He frowns, which makes me feel bad.

"His bones are healing quickly," Tara turns around to say. "He will soon swim."

"Tell that to my dad," Chase says.

I know he's kidding, but Tara takes him seriously. She stops and draws us into one of the boarded-up rooms. The plywood over the window has split, so a shaft of light cuts in, dividing her from us in the shadows.

"I cannot speak with your father. You must not tell him about me."

He seems thrown off by her words and by the way she watches him intently. "What . . . ?" He cocks his head.

"Your father knows many things," she says. "He cannot know about *me*."

Even I think it's odd that's she's so insistent about his dad. Then I remember his dad is a writer. A thought hits me. "Does it have something to do with running away?"

"You're running away?" Chase shouts.

"Shh!" I hiss.

"You're running away?" he repeats, this time more quietly.

His eyes are as big as pancakes as he waits for her answer. I stare at her too. I want to hear more.

She nods.

"Why?" He's asking the questions I'd like to ask but am afraid to. I don't want to scare her off.

She shakes her head. "Something happened." A terrible, sad look takes over her face.

Fear strikes through my heart. My forehead wrinkles with concern and I lean toward her. "What happened?"

For a second, her whole face crumples, and she presses her eyes hard with both hands. "Ah," she says, looking at her palms. "Tears." She shakes her head again, takes a huge breath, and lets it out slowly while closing her eyes.

"Tara—"

"Trust me," she says. "I'm trusting you." Then she looks at Chase. "I'm trusting you too."

He nods as if he knows exactly what she's talking about. She turns back to me and puts her hand on my arm.

That shiver again. Her touch. Questions crowd my mind: What happened? Did someone get hurt?

As if she could read my mind, she says, "No one was hurt. Things just . . . changed. I can never go home now."

I wait, but she doesn't say anything else.

30

Chase

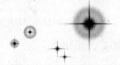

"Isn't that wild about Tara?" I ask, licking the chocolate ice cream as it melts. Allie Jo and I are sitting on a little porch in back of the hotel's ice cream place; we're taking a break from the brass. Some pigeons strut around, no doubt waiting on the bread Allie's brought in a bag.

"Yeah," she says, eating ice cream from a cup. Her advantage: she can eat it slowly. My advantage: I can eat with one hand. She takes a spoonful, swallows, and looks at me. "Have you ever thought about running away?"

I was seven years old. We'd spent the whole week in school making stuff for Mother's Day. "Bring in your mom's picture," Mrs. Harris, my first-grade teacher, had said, "and we'll paste it on the pots."

I raised my hand. "What if you don't have a mom?"

Her face collapsed. I didn't know it then, but of course

all the teachers knew about that; she'd just forgotten. Rushing to my desk, she put her hand on my shoulder and bent down to my level. "You can bring in a picture of your dad," she said cheerfully.

"Dads don't want flowers!" I knocked the pot off my desk. If it had been clay, it would've broken into a million pieces.

She picked up the plastic pot and said, "He'll love it." Then she clapped her hands at some other boys who were fooling around.

The tissue paper was dumb, only girl colors—mint green, soft pink, baby blue. I took some sheets of green, darkened them with a marker, and carefully cut the edges into three pointy shapes. A black pipe cleaner served as the stem.

Mrs. Harris waded through our desks, making admiring noises. "Roses," "daffodils," "daisies," my classmates answered brightly when she asked about their cotton candy flowers.

Then she arrived at my desk. "Chase!" She did not sound pleased. "You were supposed to make flowers. What is that?"

I looked around the room at their stupid flowers. "Poison ivy," I said.

A few kids laughed. I squinted my eyes at them and made them shut up.

"No," she said, lifting my perfectly made plant from the desk. "You need to follow instructions." After putting my poison ivy in her closet, she came back to me with pink, yellow, and blue tissue paper. "Even dads like pretty things."

On the way home, I threw it into a creek.

"Yeah," I say to Allie Jo now. "I've thought about running away before."

She's down to the bottom scoop in her cup. She plays with her spoon, then looks at me. "Did you ever do it?"

I shake my head.

"Why not?"

I shrug. "I didn't want to leave my dad alone."

She seems to think about that as we finish our ice cream. She grabs the bag of bread, hands me a few slices, and we start tossing shreds out. The pigeons flock in, the bigger ones pushing out the smaller ones.

Leaning forward on her rocking chair, Allie Jo asks, "Why do you think Tara ran away?"

"I don't know." I don't know why people run away.

A fat pigeon with angry eyes waddles closer. He looks like a general. I give him a piece of crust. Pigeons have pink legs. No wonder he's so mad.

"How come birds fly south for the winter?" she asks in a singsong voice.

I groan. "Okay, how come?"

She throws out a handful of bread, trying to reach the smaller birds in back. "Because it's too far to walk."

I drop my head, shake it, then look at her. "Allie Jo, we need to get you some new material."

31

Allie Jo

Instead of having us finish the brass, Dad sets a box of flyers for Taste of Hope on the desk and asks me to deliver it to Mrs. Brimble. "Here you go," he says, handing me some money. I count it and see he's given enough for both Chase and me to ride the bus and get lemonades.

But Chase doesn't want to ride the bus. That's how I end up on his skateboard while he carries the box.

Why, oh, why did I agree to a skateboarding lesson?

"I can't do this!" I yell.

"Yes, you can!" he hollers back.

I'm riding the skateboard down the main boulevard. It's just a little bit of a hill, but, believe me, that's enough. Every crack and every stone in the sidewalk tries to bump me off, which they almost do, but even though I'm wobbling, I'm still on.

Finally, the ground levels out and I hop off.

"What are you doing?" Chase asks. He's not out of breath even though he's been jogging this whole time. A sheen of sweat covers his face, but if anything, he seems like he's got more energy, not less.

"I'm getting off," I say. "There's no more hill."

Chase grins. "You can't depend on hills for skateboarding. You have to make your own motion." He hands the box to me, hops on the board, and pushes a few times with his foot; he's gliding. It looks so easy when he does it. Then he pops the board up, grabs it, and looks back at me. "See?"

He waits while I catch up to him. The bus passes us, blowing hot exhaust on me. I watch all those air-conditioned seats breeze by.

Boy, am I glad I've got that money. A tall glass of lemonade is what I'm after. "Are you supposed to be riding that skateboard?" I ask.

"I'm not riding it," he says. "I'm just showing you stuff." He takes the box back. "Try again."

Sighing, I plant my right foot squarely on the board and pump with my left. Surprisingly, skateboarding over level ground is easier than riding down the hill. I think it has something to do with control.

"Doing good!" Chase yells behind me.

This is all right. Better than walking, for two reasons:

number one, it's faster; number two, I'm making my own breeze by sailing on the board.

When we get up to the intersection, I put my foot down to stop, but my flip-flop curls under and I scrape my toes on the concrete. I stumble and fall off—visions of getting run over hit me—and the board skitters off the curb and gets stuck in a grate. Someone pounds their car horn at me while making the turn. It sounds like, *Dummy! You're a dummy!*

"Idiots," Chase says as he catches up to me. "You all right?"

My knee and ankle are scratched up, but there's only a little bit of blood. Now I can understand how he got hurt. "I'm kinda done with this," I say. "Besides, Brimble's is right there."

He glances across the street, and I grin, knowing I'm saved.

A chain of bells tinkles as we open Brimble's door. Ah, air-conditioning. The bells are really Christmas décor; so are the white lights lining most roofs and porches downtown. It's part of what gives this place so much character.

"Hello, Allie Jo." Old Mrs. Brimble comes out from her sitting area. She's got a TV back there and a couple of comfy chairs. "You have something for me?"

"Yes, ma'am." I hand her the box with stuff for the festival.

"I don't believe I've met you before, young man." Her eyes twinkle at Chase.

He cocks a smile and looks at her through his hair, which he flips out of his eyes.

"I'm Chase," he says, extending his hand across the counter.

"Oh, well"—Mrs. Brimble stretches her own hand and shakes his—"aren't you something?"

Chase laughs and looks down at his feet before looking up. "Thank you," he says.

I tell her we want two ice-cold lemonades, but before I can pay, Chase pulls some bills from his pocket and puts the change in the tip jar.

"Well!" Mrs. Brimble says; then, in a stage whisper, "I like your young man!"

"What? He's not my—"

"It's okay, honey. You enjoy those lemonades!" Her eyes sparkle like she knows something.

I frown as I turn away from the counter, but Chase smirks.

"It's not funny," I say. "She thought we were boyfriend and girlfriend."

"That's why it's funny," Chase says.

He starts for a table, but I head for the door. "Let's sit outside," I say. I don't want any more of Mrs. Brimble's lovey-dovey talk. The bells tinkle after us.

We sit on white rockers and sip our lemonade. Fans spin lazily over our heads. One thing about Mrs. Brimble— she's a hard worker. None of her tables or chairs are sticky, and that's a challenge when you're running an ice-cream store.

A few cars pass through the light as it changes. People, mostly ladies, stroll along the sidewalk with fancy boutique bags.

"Uh-oh." I shrink into my rocker.

"What?" Chase leans forward. "What?"

"Don't look at them," I say. "But see those three girls coming? They're from my school."

Chase looks confused. "So? Don't you want to say hi to them?"

Jennifer, Heather, and Lori—the top girls in school. "I can't say hi to them—they're the *popular* people."

He shakes his head like I'm the one confused. So I say, "They kick my backpack and one of them slapped my shoulder because I sat in the bus seat she was saving. I didn't even know she was saving it."

They're getting closer. Too late to run back in; I turn my head to Chase. "Pretend like we're talking, okay?" I put my lemonade down. I don't want to be sucking on a straw when they pass.

"I hate people like that," Chase says.

My whole body tenses. "They might hear you!"

Then he laughs like I've just told the funniest joke he ever heard in the whole world. He flashes his eyebrows at me, and then I realize he wants me to laugh too, so I do. Except I make my laugh not as loud as his, since I am the one who supposedly told the joke.

"Hi, Allie Jo," Jennifer says. She's talking to me? They stop dead in front of us. Jennifer smiles like she's in a toothpaste commercial.

I narrow my eyes. "Hi."

"Who's your friend?" She turns her Medusa eyes on me.

I hate giving information to the enemy. I mutter, "Chase."

Her face becomes as sunny as a daisy and she turns it, probably trying to show her best side—not that she even has one—and says, "Hi, Chase!"

"H'lo." He acts polite but NOT INTERESTED.

Then she starts talking, sweet like syrup, as if she and I have always been friends.

Heather and Lori get in on it too, all *How's your summer?* and *What have you been up to?* like they've never snickered behind my back.

"You should invite us up sometime," Jennifer says. She looks directly at Chase. He tosses the hair out of his eyes, and I swear, those girls practically melt.

"Well, I—"

"We have to go now." Jennifer links arms with Heather and Lori, and they fall into each other, giggling as they walk away. Jennifer looks over her shoulder at Chase, probably knowing how her long, blond hair spills just right over her bare shoulder. "See you later."

He nods at her, which sends her into titters, and they disappear around the corner.

I cross my arms and slam back into my rocker. "I hate them! They're so fake."

"Who cares about them?" Chase asks.

"Not me," I say. And I don't. What bothers me is the way Jennifer acts like she's got a big secret over us mere mortals.

Mrs. Brimble comes out holding a glass of iced tea. "You wouldn't mind if an old lady joins you, would you, now?"

We laugh.

"You're not an old lady!" Well, she is, but still, I would rather be sitting with an old lady than be put down by a bunch of stuck-up girls.

She sets herself down beside us. "You're not from here, are you?" she asks Chase.

I watch him as he gives his carefully worded answers about his family. His face does not give him away at all, like he's had lots of practice lying about his mom. Though when he looks back at me, his eyes glitter with the truth.

32

Chase

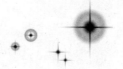

Allie Jo and I sit on the backseat of the city bus. Every-one knows the best ride is in the back—you get all the bumps. "Thanks for not saying anything about my mom."

She nods. "How do bees get to school?" she asks. "On the school buzz." When I don't laugh, she looks down at her hands, folded in her lap. Then she asks, "What's it like not having a mom?"

I take a big breath and sigh. "I don't know." How would I? Nothing to compare it with. "It's kind of an empty house, you know. I'm alone a lot."

She acts like she knows what I'm talking about. "I don't have a lot of friends either."

"I didn't say I don't have a lot of friends; I said I don't have a mother."

Good going, Chase. I can see the hurt in Allie Jo's eyes.

"Why did the turkey cross the road?" I ask.

She rolls her eyes at me.

"He didn't," I say. "He was too chicken."

"Ha, ha," she says.

I elbow her. "C'mon, you know you'll be telling that one later."

She goes, "I do have friends, you know. Just not a whole bunch. And definitely not those girls we saw."

"That's why you wanted to ride the bus, right? You didn't want those girls to see you. You're hiding."

Her mouth opens and an expression crosses her face before she switches on an angry look. Too late; I already saw it—the look of truth.

"You shouldn't be bothered by them. Why do you even care?"

"Because they're *popular*." Her eyes bug out, like this means something.

The bus stops and picks up two dudes wearing skull-caps and black T-shirts. Warm air whooshes in when the door closes after them. They pass us; one dude nods at me after seeing my skateboard.

"Those girls probably pick their noses when no one's looking and breathe in each other's farts." I crack up. Boogers and butts usually work, but farts are *always* funny. Allie Jo must be picturing it too because she starts laughing.

"Hey," she says, "are you coming to Taste of Hope? Sophie will be there."

"Sophie's going?"

She smiles. "She's helping me pass out samples." Then she slaps her leg. "You should help too! It's really fun and there're all kinds of food, which you get for free of course, and some places even give stuff out like little flashlights or key chains and—"

"Yeah, yeah! I'll come." It sounds like fun. Besides, "Does Sophie like me?" Oh, dude. You totally blabbed. I try to play it cool, shift my skateboard and stuff. I steal a glance at Allie Jo.

"I can't tell you," she says, doing that lip-scrunching thing girls do. "I never tell secrets."

I nod and don't say another word, but if she can't tell me, that means only one thing—Sophie *does* like me! A weird sensation floods my chest and I suddenly feel like I do when I'm flying off a ramp.

I feel so good, it doesn't even bother me when we get off at the hotel and Allie Jo's mom walks off the porch and gives her a hug. It doesn't bother me at all.

33

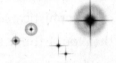

"You mind if I sit on the veranda?" I ask Mom and Dad after supper.

Mom looks at me oddly. "This is getting to be a regular habit with you. What's so interesting out there?"

My heart quickens. "Nothing! It's just relaxing, you know, moon, stars, that sort of thing." I lick my lips real quick. "So can I go?"

Mom scrapes a plate; Dad clears the milk. "Yes, go ahead," Mom says.

I give them both quick pecks and dash away before they can change their minds.

I hope I see Tara tonight. I can't stop thinking about her. Neither can Chase.

Throughout the day, we'd pieced together what we knew about her: she was from Ireland or Scotland but grew up in America; she has friends at wherever she's from; something bad happened; no one was hurt, but whatever happened, she ran away and now she can't go back home.

"And what about how she talks," Chase pointed out.

I love her accent and the lilt of her voice.

But Chase went on to say it wasn't just her accent. "It's the way she talks, like all sophisticated."

True, but I like that too. I think it makes her sound wise and knowing. She doesn't speak like a normal teenager, but I guess that's because she isn't from around here.

I told him my stepmother theory on why Tara was running away and how that could explain why she has only one outfit.

He shook his head slowly, then snapped to. "It means she ran away suddenly, like not planning it."

I inhaled sharply. "Yes! Whatever happened, she had to get away right then." But for the life of me I couldn't think of anything so bad that someone would have to run away with just the clothes on her back.

I'm still wondering as I close the suite door behind me, leaving Mom and Dad behind. I steal into the service tower, slip outside, and sit by the springs. Crickets and frogs murmur into the night air.

Taking a deep breath, I lean back and let it out slowly.

I wonder what it's like to be a runaway.

The springhead bubbles and I kick the water. Images of Tara coming out of the springs flit through my mind: Tara slicing through the water that first afternoon I saw her, and later, Tara emerging from the moonlit springs.

Clouds pass over the moon.

I rise slowly. My toes curl over the edge of the dock. Then I jump.

I plunge into the ice-cold water, bubbles and movement swirling around me. My whole system is in shock. When my toes feel the pebbly bottom, I push off underwater, toward the depths of the springhead. I expect to glide like Tara, but my clothes billow and catch water, weighing me down. Strands of algae curl around my foot. I shriek underwater, losing important oxygen.

Something coarse and bristly touches me. I jerk away and bump into another creature. It squeals as we touch. My heart explodes in panic. Currents rush past me in thunderous roars. I can't tell which way is up or down. My lungs strain for air. I push my arms down, but dark shapes float above me through the moonlight.

The shapes chirp and grunt, push me up with their flippers. Flinching, I accidentally send myself deeper.

Then I hear a loud crash—the sound of someone, or some*thing*, jumping into the springs. The trilling gets louder and more excited. Suddenly, a pair of hands—not flippers— grabs me under the arms. We shoot to the top, my lungs bursting as we surface. I wheeze and suck in air before turning to face my rescuer.

"Tara!"

Her face glows from within, but her expression, which I notice now, is a mix between concern and anger. We drift to the dock and climb out. I'm gasping for air. I collapse in a heap, not quite sure of what happened to me down there.

She grabs a couple of towels off the cabinet, hands one to me, and sits.

Her eyes flash under dark eyebrows. "What were you doing?"

My chest heaves. The roar of the springs still sounds in my ear. "I don't know," I say. I don't know why I jumped in. Yes, I do. "I wanted to be like you." I shiver and pull the towel around me.

"But you're not like me."

That kind of hurts my feelings. "I know you probably have all kinds of friends back home and you're prettier than me, but—"

"Allie Jo"—she leans closer to me—"you have good skin." She pinches my cheeks and pulls my nose.

I curl away and giggle.

"It fits you well." Her face softens. "Aren't you comfortable in it?"

"Well, yeah, but . . ." Even Mom says I need to be more

comfortable in my own skin. But no one calls *her* hotel rat. "Sometimes I think it would be easier to be invisible."

Tara shakes her head. "You wouldn't want to be invisible," she says seriously. "People bump into you all the time and no one talks to you."

I stare at her for a second, and then I start laughing. She tilts her head and laughs too.

"Well, come on then," she says, pulling herself up. "You'll want to put on some dry clothes."

As I stand up, my legs wobble. I remember the roar of the springs. "I almost drowned! Something was in there!" Shuddering, I rub my arms where that bristly . . . *thing* touched me.

"Manatees," she says, leading the way to the hotel. "They meant no harm."

"No harm!" I jog to catch up to her. "They were pushing me around."

Tara giggles. "Sea cows."

As we cross the lawn, I think about my favorite pajamas and my nice cozy bedroom and the cup of hot chocolate I'll make for myself. I glance at Tara, soaking wet in her only outfit because she had to jump in and save me.

"How did you know I was in the water?"

Her lips suggest a smile without actually making one. She puts her arm around my shoulders and touches her head to mine. It makes me feel so good.

My heart swells and at the same time suffers a pang. Who made her run away? Is she lonely? Is she scared? I can't imagine her being frightened of anything; she's so brave.

Where does she sleep at night? As we near the hotel, I realize I've never asked her. Well, I'm about to fix that right now.

34

Chase

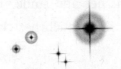

Dad and I are watching some old Western and decide the only thing that can make it watchable is popcorn. I head out to the first-floor vending machine and spot Sophie doing the same thing.

"We've got to stop meeting like this," I say. Yes! Good one.

Instead of sticking her money in, she leans against the wall. Suddenly, I'm overwhelmed by the sensation of falling into her, but I catch myself before I do. "Sophie," I say.

"Yes?"

She looks up at me, causing my heart to race, but I'm not nervous. A sure current pulses through my body and I feel like I'm on another planet. I reach out and smooth her hair like I'd wanted to the other day. When my hand touches her throat, I feel her heart beating as fast as mine.

I kiss her. Oh, my God, I kiss her. Her lips are soft and strawberry and her arms go around my neck. It's better than I ever imagined, and it's over way too soon.

The next breath I take is pure satisfaction. My eyelids feel heavy. I look at her and smile. "You're so pretty." I want to stroke her hair, touch her cheek. I want to kiss her again.

Her eyes sweep downward. "Thank you."

A sudden thought crosses my mind. "You don't have a boyfriend at home, do you?"

She shakes her head.

I am one lucky dude.

"I'd better get back," she says. "My mom will come out looking for me!"

She starts to turn and I touch her arm lightly. "You forgot to get your popcorn."

One hand flies up to her mouth and her face turns pink.

"I've never kissed anybody before," she says.

"Me neither."

We stare at each other.

Down the hall, a door creaks open. "Sophie?" her mom calls out. She waves. "Hi, Chase!"

I wave back. *I just kissed your daughter!*

Afterward, I float back to the room with the popcorn. "Hi, Dad," I say, even though he's on the phone. I feel like I did when the doctor set my arm—warm and far away, like I'm not really here. It seems like someone else's hands that toss the popcorn into the microwave.

As I flop onto the bed, I hear Dad laugh as he tells a story about us. It's not even the words, just the sound of his voice. The popcorn is popping and Dad is laughing. Everything's good.

"Gail?" I ask when he hangs up the phone.

"Yeah." He clears his throat and gets up for the timer. "Mmm, cheesy. Smells good." He pops open the bag and holds it toward me.

I shake my head. "I'm good." I could not be better.

And when I look at him, I see a curious smile on his face.

"What?" I ask.

He snaps straight. "What?"

I relax against the pillow. "Nothing."

"Okay," he says, and his eyes lose their focus.

He sits against his headboard and I prop myself up to catch the end of the movie. We're right at the part where the good guy wins.

35

Tara and I are in the tunnels, dank passageways that crawl under the hotel in every direction. Crumbling bricks line the entrance tunnel, hidden from public view by sloping gardens. Gliding underground into the semidarkness, I feel something like a runaway myself. Mist from the springs wraps around me, making my skin dewy. A slight mildew smell floats in the air. I hear the *drip, drip, drip* of a leak.

When we hit the service area, the tunnel splinters off into a bunch of different smaller shafts. Rough wooden staircases start up, then turn; you can't see from the ground where they lead to. Tall, skinny doors shut off some paths. Workers still use these tunnels, but mainly as a shortcut to get to the parking lot or the springs. That's why I'm walking on my toes. If anyone is down here, I want to hear them before they hear me.

When we reach the service tower, I motion for Tara to follow me. I expect her to look scared, like Melanie does when I bring her down here at night, but Tara slides her hand along the wall and her face is full of wonderment.

Well, of course she wouldn't be scared. She's been staying in a maid's closet upstairs where there are no lights—she's obviously not afraid of the dark.

We head up the tower stairs, which are wide on account of the porters having to carry those trunks through here and deliver them to the proper rooms, all without being seen. I stick my head up to the porthole on the first-floor landing. All clear.

I turn to Tara. "Stay here," I whisper. My heart's beating faster than a hummingbird's wings. I turn the knob, wincing at its metallic click, then scamper across the hall to the front desk and pull a little key from under the countertop. The front desk closes at ten, so Clay and Dad are gone. Even so, I hurry. I unlock the wide cedar cabinet behind me; more than half the keys hang inside. Which room? I lift the key for 201. Being on the north corner, it's got two views of the parking lot. I'm pretty sure no one's got reservations for it.

"Freeze!" someone barks. The voice is commanding enough that I do. I am a frozen statue, my heart pounding like a kettledrum. Then he laughs.

I purse my eyebrows. "Chase, that's not funny." I stalk past him.

He falls in behind me. "Where you going?" He's holding two cans of soda. "Why are you all wet?"

"Shh!" For all my sneaking around, he's talking right out loud, about to give me up without even knowing it.

His voice is surprised when we slip through the door of the service tower. "Tara!"

She at least has the good sense to say hello quietly.

The darkness in the tower covers our movements. We tiptoe close to the rails so no creaks can give us away.

"What are we doing?" Chase whispers.

How did this get to be *we*? "*I'm* putting Tara in a room," I say. "Now be quiet!"

I check for all clear on the second-floor landing, motion to Tara and Chase, and cut to 201.

"Whoa!" Chase glances around once we're inside, then looks at Tara. "Your own room! Cool."

I say, "Well, at least for tonight." Even one night seems risky, but she deserves the comfort. "Is that root beer?" I ask him. "I sure am thirsty."

He glances down at the root beer, then reluctantly hands it over.

I pop it open and drink a big swig.

"May I have some?" Tara asks. "I'm thirsty too."

She wrinkles her nose as she lifts the can to her

mouth, then takes a small, careful sip. "What spirits are these?"

"What?" Chase and I say together.

"This drink—it bubbles and boils." She looks at us plainly. "What spell does it cast?"

My lips part in confusion.

"Watch and see!" Chase grabs the can from Tara, downs about half of it, then lets out a huge belch.

"Gross!" I say and throw a pillow at him. He laughs. I turn to Tara. "Don't you drink soda?"

She shakes her head. "We don't have soda where I'm from. I don't think I like it."

Chase heads for the door. "I gotta get going. My dad's waiting on this pop."

"Don't let anyone see you," I say. "Look through the crack first."

He waves me off. "I got it," he says, then slips out.

I'd better get going too; Mom and Dad will be wondering where I am. Quickly, I show Tara how to use the TV and the shower. I set the TV to a program I like, something that might make Tara laugh.

When I get back to my own suite, Mom and Dad are sitting on the couch, watching the same show.

"Have a nice time?" Mom asks, then leans back. Her mouth drops in horror, the kind of horror only moms can have. "You're all wet!"

Dad whips his head around. He stares at me, waiting, like Mom.

"I . . . went swimming." What else can I say?

Mom's horror intensifies. "At night? Were the pool lights on? Was anyone else there?"

They think I went in the pool. "I'm sorry." I feel like I'm lying, but I'm not. I never said I jumped into the pool.

She comes around the couch and stares at me with mom eyes. "You didn't ask us if you could go swimming. What if something had happened?"

Coarse and bristly shapes dart through my mind.

Mom puckers her eyebrows. "Allie Jo?"

"Nothing happened," I say, almost pleading, because I don't want to talk about this anymore. "I was safe."

"You know better than to swim at night without someone around."

Someone *was* around, but I can't say that. I look straight at her. "I'm sorry." I try to emphasize it. I *am* sorry, but at the same time, something happened tonight, something bigger than me swimming at night without permission. I want to be left alone so I can think about it.

Dad steps up. "Well, go take a shower and put your pj's on," he says, sighing. "And dry up that puddle you're making."

I look down and, sure enough, water trickles from my clothes, down my legs, and onto the floor. I pull the towel from around my shoulders, sop up the water, and dash past Mom and Dad to the bathroom. My bones feel loosey-goosey, like noodles. No wonder, after all the excitement tonight.

I face the shower, let the hot water pour over me. For all that batting around, there're no scratches on my arms. Sea cows, I think, and try to laugh like Tara did. But I can't. I'd been terrified. If she hadn't dived in when she did—I don't even want to think about it. I turn my back to the water and close my eyes.

36

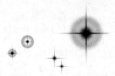

She'd seen the magic box before. The man had had one—TV, that's what they called it—but he kept his dark. Instead, he filled the air with endless schemes as to how he would use her to get into the magic box and make "buttloads" of money. She did not know how much a buttload was, but she gleaned a sense from the man that it was far greater than he had now.

Tara glanced around at her present surroundings. Allie Jo said she would be safe here, showing her the bathroom and how to work something called a remote. Walking behind Allie Jo, she'd picked up a new sense in the air the girl had passed through. Love, or something like it. She trailed her fingertips where Allie Jo had touched the walls; she felt . . . security . . . salvation. Yes, she thought now, alone in the room, she'd been right about Allie Jo.

She'd been right about Chase too. He was a kindred spirit.

What a magnificent thrum he'd produced after drinking the soda!

She flopped onto the bed, so bouncy! She grasped a pillow and hugged it to herself. Everything was soft. Perhaps humans made things that way because the earth itself was so very hard.

The people on the magic box sat on a couch. Could they see her? Still squeezing the pillow, she sat up and leaned forward. They spoke only to each other. A new person came in through a door. How did they do this? She looked behind the magic box and spied a long, black cord. The wee folk must walk to and fro in the cord, gathering in the magic box. Unlike the man, she had no desire to go into the magic box; what if she got stuck?

Moving to the front of the TV—for she decided she must use the human word for it—she watched the TV people talk. They looked everywhere except straight at her. She rapped on the glass. A crowd of people laughed, hundreds of them! She dropped to the floor in fright, her heart pounding. Crawling, she reached the other side of the bed and peered over the edge. No crowd appeared on the TV, but she had distinctly heard them. The TV people carried on as though nothing had happened.

This box disturbed her. Looking at the remote, she saw all kind of buttons and markings; she was about to turn the power off—and here again she marveled that humans could wield such power over the wee folk—when, suddenly, a woman appeared in a bathroom.

Squeezing a liquid into her hands, the woman made bubbles in her hair. Doing so caused the woman to smile with great joy. Tara watched until the other people came back into the box. Then she turned the power off. She didn't want the wee folk wandering about when she had her back turned.

In the bathroom, she came upon bottles not unlike the one the woman had. Her heart thrilled! She would partake of this joy. She uncapped the bottle. A sweet scent wafted up, tickling her nose, and she understood this was a potion. She couldn't wait to get into the water.

Tomorrow, she would see Allie Jo again. Allie Jo had promised to bring her breakfast, something called blueberry pancakes.

She hoped it tasted like fish.

37

Chase

Dad's schedule is loose this morning, so I take him out to the springs.

"Hot already," Dad says. When we sit on the concrete, he takes off his sandals; the shape of them is branded in a crispy sunburn on Dad's red feet.

"Stick your feet in," I say. "They'll feel better."

He plunks his feet into the water. "Oh!"

I laugh.

"Look." Dad gestures to the only other people out here, an old couple.

The lady is inching her way down the concrete steps; the lower she goes, the higher she hunches her shoulders. A white bathing cap makes her look bald. Then she straightens her arms in front of her and goes under with a little jump. She pops up and whoops.

"Guess it's not the fountain of youth," Dad says. He leans over and points. "An egret!"

He scans the horizon, and I feel him drift away from me. He's doing it again—narrating the scene. I bet it sounds like this: *It was a cool*—wait!—*a* balmy *morning when I sat with my son at the mouth of the fountain of youth. An egret fished nearby, while hopeful tourists bathed in the springs, praying Ponce de León was right.*

"Earth to Dad."

He answers without looking at me. "Yeah?"

"Dad!" I kick up some water. "I'm trying to talk to you."

He looks at me, but he's not quite focused. *The ever-present bubbling of the springs, while not restoring youth, rejuvenated her soul, which before had ached with the pain of life.*

"Dad? Dad!"

His pupils shrink. Finally, he's come to the surface. "What?" He grins. He knows I've caught him. "Yeah, yeah," he says. "What do you want to do today? Go to a movie? A museum?"

Yes, museums—top of my list, right under malls and church.

I tap my feet on the water's surface, causing little fish to dart away. "I don't know." A lizard is not two feet from my hand, blowing out a red sack under his neck. "Dad, look!"

He leans to see around me. When he does, I catch sight of Sophie and her parents walking out to the pool.

"Sophie!" I bellow. So much for playing it cool. I raise my left hand and wave. "Sophie!"

I can see her smile from here.

"Hi, Chase!" She does that little finger toodle girls do.

"That's how the males attract the females," Dad says.

"What?" I whip around, caught in the act.

"The lizard," Dad says, a cockeyed grin taking over his face. "What did you think I was talking about?"

"Nothing," I say. But I can't help grinning back.

Dad and I were still thinking about what to do when, out of nowhere, it started storming. As we ran in through the dining room, I turned and saw Sophie and her family running in by the pool.

That's why I didn't mind at all when Dad said a nap sounded good.

"Go ahead, Dad," I assured him. "You need it."

He headed up the stairs and I pretended not to see Sophie and her parents as I made my way toward them. I put my finger to my chin, hoping to look interested in the old black-and-white photographs on the walls: "Clark Gable Enjoying The Meriwether's Famous Blueberry Pancakes," "Construction Site, 1887," "Hope Springs Eternal."

"Chase!"

I turn from the photos and act surprised. "Hey! The rain get you?"

"It's pouring!" Sophie unlinks arms with her mom and smiles up at her. "Okay if I hang out?"

My heart does a little zing.

After her parents leave, I shove my hand into my pocket. "Knit anything lately?" Way to be a dweeb, Chase! Geez!

"Actually, I knit every day," she says. Her eyes twinkle.

"That sounds good," I say. I think about our kiss last night. "Allie Jo told me you're helping with Taste of Hope."

"She told me you are too." She looks at me shyly from under her eyelashes.

"Well," I say. "Maybe we should go report to the boss."

It's only a short way from where we are to the front desk, but I feel every second of it. I'm aware of how I walk and how I smile, and when we look at each other, a hum goes through me. I reach for her hand.

An old couple passes us in the hallway, and they smile at us. Oh, man, is it that obvious? My face is probably all lit up with a goofy grin, big doofus, but when we pass more photographs and I look at our reflection, I see a girl and a normal boy.

I stick my chest out and smile at my reflection.

38

Allie Jo

I've filed all the vendor accounts and dusted Dad's office, including his desk, the pictures on the wall, and even the baseboards. Brass is next. Polishing brass is part of my regular chores, of course, but everything else I was forced to do as part of my punishment.

The morning started off all right; I woke up before Mom and Dad, left a note on the counter, and slipped out the door. Chef opens the breakfast buffet early on Saturdays and Sundays for the weekend travelers, and that worked out especially well for me because no one was on hand to see my leaning tower of blueberry pancakes and packets of syrup, which I whisked upstairs through the tunnels and up the north nanny staircase.

"Tara, it's me," I whispered, putting my mouth right up to the corner where the door meets the frame. I shot a look down the hall; after all, I did live on this very same floor, just all the way down. "Tara!" I kicked the door softly, my hands being full.

The door opened and I saw a sliver of her through the crack.

Her eyes crinkled with a smile. "Allie Jo!" The door shut and I heard her rattle the chain off before she opened it again.

I slipped in real quick, brandishing The Meriwether's Famous Blueberry Pancakes. Steam rose off them in disappearing swirls, and the butter melted like rays of sunshine down the stack.

"Breakfast," I said, "is served!"

We sat at the desk, and I opened the to-go packet with a napkin, a fork, and a knife in it, folding up the napkin fancy so she'd know this is a five-star breakfast. I slipped out the extra plate and set up a place for myself.

She breathed in heavily. "It smells sweet, like nectar."

"That's the blueberries," I said, tearing open a syrup packet.

She watched me, then did the same.

I took the first bite, letting the blueberry goodness explode in my mouth.

Tara stared at me.

Motioning with my fork, I said, "Eat 'em while they're hot!"

With careful movements, she cut her pancakes, tapped them in the syrup, and put a bite in her mouth. "Hmm," she said, keeping her lips closed.

"I know," I said around a mouthful of pancake, then clamped my lips shut. I didn't want her to think I ate like a pig.

She finished that stack awfully quick and looked like she could eat some more, which got me to wondering if she'd been eating at all. I watched her rub her finger on her plate and lick the syrup off. I guess we are alike in some things.

With a satisfied belly and the good feeling I had from bringing her breakfast, I felt warm and cozy, like in a dream. Tara's manners were excellent, and I bet by the way she talked, she got As in English. Thoughts of school crowded in, even though I tried to push them out. I got As in English, but if it came to friends, I'd get an F. No, I'd get the kind of grade Melanie gets in PE—Doesn't Participate.

I put my hands between my knees and leaned forward against the desk. "Do you have a best friend?" I asked her.

She nodded. "Lots of them."

My shoulders slumped. "Oh."

"Why?" she asked, and licked the syrup from her pointer, middle, and ring fingers. "Do you have a best friend?"

"Melanie," I said, slumping even more. "But she's on vacation for the rest of the summer."

She stopped with the syrup and looked right at me. "What about your other friends?"

I looked right back at her, right at the way she peered into my eyes, and I knew I couldn't lie; I couldn't even fudge the truth. Looking down, I said, "I don't really have any other friends."

I explained to her about how I ride the bus for a long way to school and how the closest other girls are Jennifer Jorgensen and her friends and how mean Jennifer is to me. "And I've never done anything to her," I said. "But every time I see her, she either ignores me or says something and then she and her friends laugh at me. They're always with her."

Tara leaned forward. "You are very strong. They come together against you because, alone, they cannot match you."

Of course, this made me feel better. And when I thought about it, I couldn't even picture Jennifer without her followers. But still . . . she's Jennifer Jorgensen.

"Test her," Tara said. "Test her when she's alone."

"Well, that's not the only thing." Then I explained the story of my life to her. How my dad has only a two-year college degree, and how my mom graduated high school, got married, and before you know it, I came along. They met while working here—Mom waitressing,

Dad bellhopping—and I guess we just naturally worked our way into the hotel family.

Most of the kids in school have parents who work in tall buildings in the downtowns of nearby cities. And you can be sure they don't live in those same buildings.

A lot of people at school think it's weird I live in a hotel. They say hotels are just for vacations or weekends. Some people feel sorry for me, like I don't have a real home. Hardly any of them consider the fact that I *like* living here. I'd hate to live in one of those subdivisions where the houses all look the same and the only thing that makes them different is the house number. Do any of them live over tunnels or have secret staircases? Do any of them walk outside to crystal water bubbling from a deep underground cavern? Can any of them say they live in a five-star home?

But they don't think about that stuff. Not even the grown-ups, who're split between looking at The Meriwether as a historical jewel or wanting to declare the place condemned and raze it, which is a weird word because it sounds like you're building something up but the whole time it means tearing it down.

Tara sat straight as an arrow. "Knock it down?" Her eyes rounded with shock. "What of their fathers? The ghosts of the past are in these walls—I can feel them."

Then she looked shocked again, as if what she just said surprised her.

But I totally agreed.

I wondered if this was how it felt between Isabelle and Karen, talking about stuff and having the same feelings. Tara is so wise. I bet she'd make an excellent sister.

Housekeeping would be around soon, and I couldn't let them find Tara in the room. As soon as we were done talking, I poked my head out, saw the all clear, and let her run across to the north staircase. Then I shut the door. She'd been a neat guest, no towels on the floor or pillows thrown all over. You'd be surprised the shape some grown adults leave a hotel room in.

First, I threw out the plasticware, which is what you call silverware when it's plastic, the syrup packets, and one used mini shampoo bottle. Pulling the bag from the wastebasket, I tied it off neatly and grabbed the plates. I had to make up the room for the next guest.

I saw the service cart down the hall, but no housekeeper. Good. I ran down, threw the trash on it, and grabbed a new shampoo bottle. Back in the room, I neatened everything up and wiped everything down—I like doing a good job—and the last item of business was stripping the bed.

With all the sheets and pillowcases, my arms were full. I opened the door, but it wanted to shut on me, so

I held it open with my butt, struggled out with my load, turned, and found myself face-to-face with Mary, one of our housekeepers.

Next thing I knew, I was sitting on the vinyl couch behind the closed doors of Dad's office. "What were you doing in there?" Dad yelled. Not loud, but for Dad, it was practically shouting. "You know you're not allowed to use the guest rooms." He pressed his lips together and stared at me.

He'd never looked at me with that expression before. I tried to return his gaze, but his disappointment was too crushing. I tucked my chin into my shoulder. "I'm sorry."

"Did you take your friends in there?"

Without looking up, I shook my head.

He wanted to know why I changed the sheets, why there was trash to throw out, and what I was doing in there in the first place.

I bit my lip and stared at him. I had no answers. Tears filled my eyes, but my mouth stayed shut. I made a promise and I was going to keep it. Adults wouldn't understand about Tara—they'd have to *do* something about her; that much I knew.

I couldn't let that happen.

Dad looked down and shook his head. "You're in trouble, Allie Jo. You realize that, right?"

I nodded. My chin trembled a little. Though I sat on his couch and he sat on his chair, I felt like there was a big space between us.

He watched me, not with anger, but with love. That's the part that bothered me the most, that he hoped for me to say something that would close the gap.

A minute or two went by before he said anything, and when he did, it was to tell me my punishment and remind me of the rules.

I *know* the rules for the hotel. But breaking them this time wasn't wrong; I know that in my heart. I just can't tell Dad. I pour the Brasso, swab the rails with one rag, wipe them clean with the other rag. Fingerprints gone. Just wipe the rails clean and they shine good as gold. Wish everything were that easy.

39

Chase

The spell is broken when we see Allie Jo at the front desk. Her hair swings in front of her face like a curtain. She's polishing the brass rails and her whole body sways left and right, like someone standing on a ship in rough water.

"Hey!" I shout, expecting her to jump out of her skin like she did last night.

Instead, she turns with what seems like her last ounce of energy. "Ha, ha," she says. "Hi, Sophie." Then she goes back to her polishing.

"What's wrong with you?" I ask at the same time Sophie's saying, "What's wrong?"

Allie Jo glances between us. "I can't say right now."

I realize she's been working without me. "Hey," I say, "you leaving any brass for me? I want to get paid today!"

Sophie whispers to Allie Jo, and Allie Jo points her to the office. "Second door," Allie Jo says.

She waits for Sophie to leave, then lowers her voice. "Tara."

Leaning in, I whisper too. "What about her?"

Glancing at the door again, she puts the rags down and leans closer to me. Then she tells me this weird story about frogs and fish and Tara leaping out of the water and later manatees bumping her around and Tara saving her.

Then she tells the part I know, about giving Tara a room, only the story ends with Allie Jo getting caught. Now she's being punished.

"That stinks."

"What stinks?" Sophie emerges from the office.

Allie Jo bends her head and starts polishing again. Sophie gets a quizzical look on her face.

"Oh, nothing," I say. Then, to Allie Jo: "Want some help?"

She looks up from her rags. "That would be great."

"I'll help too," Sophie says.

I grab more rags and another bottle from under the desk. As I do, I spot a pink shirt in the Lost and Found. I think of Tara and her one outfit, so I jumble the shirt with the clean rags and deposit it behind the vending machine before leading Sophie to the French doors.

"Um, I don't really know how to do this," Sophie says.

"C'mon, I'll show you."

I give her a quick lesson on brass polishing. I notice the top of her head as I talk, the part on the side, the hair that's escaped the part.

Sophie flicks her hair with her hand. "Is there a bug in my hair?"

"No," I say, and smile. "Your hair is just right."

She smiles too. I smile and she smiles. We're still smiling when Allie Jo pops up from behind the desk and calls out, "I'm sure glad I'm not paying you today."

40

Allie Jo

The moon is now missing a banana-shaped chunk. The mosquitoes aren't bad; one whines past my ear and I swat around my head.

"Sending smoke signals?" Chase asks.

I make a face at him and look across the water. After not being able to talk about Tara in front of Sophie, we agreed to meet at the springs after dark. Mom and Dad said letting me outside tonight was a trial run after the last time, so I'd better not blow it.

Chase was sure Tara would be here. "You've seen her there three times," he pointed out. Plus, he wanted to give her a shirt he stole from Lost and Found.

I told him employees weren't allowed to pick through it until after thirty days. But he shrugged me off. "Think of it as a donation," he'd said.

I look at him now, sitting expectantly with the shirt neatly folded beside him.

We sit there, the moonlight spilling on us, the water softly tugging at our feet. A lone whip-poor-will calls out. It's rare to hear one in summer; this one must have forgotten to fly back north. *Whip-poor-will! Whip-poor-will! Whip-poor-will!* No one answers him back. I wonder if he's lonely.

Suddenly, the water surges over my calves.

"Look!" Chase points across the pond.

Dark shapes stream through the shadows in the water.

I snatch my legs up and scramble backward, all the while watching.

The shapes spin and twirl, floating around each other as if they're dancing . . . or playing. I steal a glance at Chase; his eyes are locked on the springs.

The water shrieks and parts in a crashing fountain right where our feet just were.

I scream, but it's voiceless. That's how scared I am.

"Hello," Tara says, as if she didn't just scare the life out of both of us.

The watery shapes lumber away.

Her face is radiant. She climbs out of the water wearing her usual outfit. Nothing about her gives off the impression that she finds it strange for us to be here.

I notice neither Chase nor I have said anything. Tara

walks past him to the cabinet, grabs a towel, comes back, and sits on the grass.

I watch her twist and squeeze her hair, then do the same to the tail of her top.

"*What* was in that water?" Chase's voice explodes with curiosity.

"Manatees," Tara says, same way I might say *grass* if someone asked me what was green and grew on the lawn.

"Sea cows?"

Tara giggles. "They hate that name."

Chase snickers, but I'm confused. What a strange thing to say.

I gesture toward the springs. "You were swimming with them," I say, my voice full of awe.

Something strikes me to the core. "You're . . . you're . . ."

She stares at me dead on. "Yes, say it—*say it*." Her eyes penetrate mine deeply.

"A mermaid?" I say in a small voice.

Her mouth drops.

To my side, I hear Chase chuckle, then laugh openly. I look away from both of them, the tips of my ears burning. I sounded like a little girl saying that. Chase is still laughing. A mermaid. Oh, he's right. I turn back, ready to laugh at myself, but when I glance at Tara, she's staring after me with a haunted look.

41

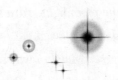

Her soul burned to name her fathers, to say aloud that which had been stripped from her. "Yes, say it—say it," she urged the girl.

Allie Jo's voice rose timorously. "A mermaid?"

Her heart crashed a hundred times upon hearing the girl's words. Humans knew only of their own legends, and even then, often did not believe. The boy laughed, but Tara did not take her eyes from the girl.

"I am Selkie." The power of the words caused her to straighten her spine.

Chase leaned over onto his elbow. "I thought you were Irish."

She spoke into the gloaming. "My fathers swam in the seas of the North and the Irish, but my own folk roam the waters of America."

The boy creased his eyebrows. "What?" he asked. She beheld

amusement in his eyes. "Are you sailors?" he asked. This, at least, seemed to be of interest to him.

"We are Selkie," she said again.

Allie Jo paled in the moonlight. Tara sensed that, although she didn't understand, she believed.

She spoke to the girl. "My skin was stolen from me as my friends and I sat upon the rocks. When the man came, my friends slipped into their skins and dove into the water, but the man snatched my skin before I could reach it."

The boy sat up, an unsure grin crossing his lips. "What skin?"

"My skin, my coat—" She searched for a phrase to make them understand. "My sealskin."

Surprised laughter escaped his lips. "Your sealskin?" With an open grin, he glanced at Allie Jo.

Confusion swirled in the twilight, curling around her. Having now told them, she must have them believe.

"Without my skin, I am human," she implored them. "With it, I return to the sea, my home." Her voice cracked saying these last words.

She saw that still they did not understand. "My people are Selkie. We live in the sea and we are clothed in sealskin. Sometimes, at night, we come ashore and take off our skins and become human so we can bask on the rocks.

"If a human man steals a Selkie woman's skin, she must become his wife. Many Selkies have been lost in this way."

Allie Jo stared at her with wide eyes. "You're a seal?"

"I am Selkie," Tara said. "But without my skin, I am human."

"Are you married?" Allie Jo asked.

"I'm too young for marriage." She brushed away tears and cast her head down. "I want to go home."

"So get your skin back," Chase said.

"I can't." Her spirit diminished upon hearing her own words.

Seeming to sense this, Allie Jo touched her arm. "What happened? Is this why you ran away? Why you can't go home?"

"My friends and I were sitting on the rocks. I strayed a bit to look for winkles, and when my friends screamed that a man was coming, I was too far.

"He watched them cloak themselves in their skins and dive into the water. They surfaced—seals now—crying out to me still. The moonlight shone on his greed. He understood perfectly what we were.

"When he saw me running, he spotted my skin and grabbed it. Then he grabbed me." Human tears filled her eyes. "It was not my hand he wanted. He said I would make money for him— that he would provide water for me and I would become a seal for him on TV."

"A magic trick," the boy said.

Tara looked at him sharply. "It is no magic; I am Selkie."

"But it's a trick, right? Like an optical illusion—he puts you in a tank and distracts the audience while you put your costume on." He grinned. "Awesome!"

Allie Jo leaned forward. "She's not joking, Chase!"

Chase glanced at the spring, then openly took Tara in. "How'd you get those manatees to swim with you?"

She stared back, measuring how to tell him. But words failed her. Instead, she stood. "Come," she said, not unkindly, for it was an invitation she bestowed. He would see with his own eyes. She held out her hand.

He rose to his feet, stood uncertainly. "You mean . . . in the springs?"

When she nodded, he said, "I'm not supposed to get my cast wet." Then his face broke with light. "But I'm getting my short cast tomorrow."

He strode up to her, his face glowing in the moonlight.

Allie Jo jumped to her feet. "Chase—"

"Your turn's next!" He grabbed Tara's hand.

Tara saw the shock on his face as she leaped into the water, taking him with her.

42

Chase

I don't know what to think. Mermaids don't exist, but maybe they do. Then again, Tara didn't say she was a mermaid; she said she was a Selkie.

I'm lying on my bed—3:00 a.m., according to the hotel clock. Dad snores on blissfully. Earlier, when I came in drenched, all he said was, *Well, I'm surprised you held out this long*, so that was cool.

But I can't sleep. Everything in me jitters; my thoughts race and my eyes stay wide open. If they plugged me in, I could light an entire city—that's how much energy courses through my body.

"Come," Tara had said, holding out her hand.

It took me a second to understand what she meant, and even then, I thought we'd jump in and her story would fizzle out as I did a one-arm dog paddle beside her.

Man, was I wrong.

She lifted me off my feet and we plunged headfirst into the springs. I barely registered the ice-cold water when Tara pushed me onto her back and torpedoed through the pond. The springs roared in my ears, made even louder by the speed of her swimming. I could feel the power of her arms, pulling us, propelling us forward.

Sounds burbled in the water, strange spaceship sounds, like electronic blips. I heard birds chirping. It was Tara—she *trilled* underwater. She slowed down and twirled us on our bellies; my heart pounded and my head was light. She turned like a dancer in the water and the sensation thrilled me. I only hoped my lungs could hold out.

Then I saw it—a sea monster, big, fat, moving slowly because it knew we couldn't escape. It stopped in front of us, a huge potato-shaped shadow. Then it opened its mouth, floated closer, and squeaked.

I screamed underwater. Tara shot to the surface with me on her back. My lungs burst. Adrenaline pumped through every vein in my body; even my feet were buzzing.

We broke through the water like a whale at SeaWorld. Gasping, I let go of her and flailed my arms, but I wasn't going anywhere.

"Chase, Chase," Allie Jo called.

Water dripped in my eyes, but I could see Allie Jo

leaning, stretching her hand over the water for me. Before I could reach her, Tara grabbed my hand, tugged me to the side, and pushed me up.

I fell onto my back and spluttered.

Allie Jo's face hovered upside down over mine. "Do you need mouth-to-mouth resuscitation?"

I squeezed my eyes shut. I heard Tara splash over the side and Allie Jo murmur to her.

I lay there catching my breath, watery images swimming past me, shadows and moonlight. My heart was finally slowing when I caught a glimpse of Tara out of the corner of my eye.

She sat straight with her legs crisscrossed, watching me.

Adrenaline shot through my nerves. My chest rose and fell quickly. Water drizzled in my eyes and I wiped them with my forearm. When I opened them again, I saw that she still looked after me, that her gaze held a yearning and a hopefulness.

I turned my head on the grass and stared at her. "That was incredible," I said.

Her eyes took on a light, as if moonbeams traveled through her.

Thinking about it now, in the dry darkness of the hotel room, I chip off pieces of my cast. I tried blow-drying it, but that was kind of useless. It had been totally worth it. A flash goes through my mind—the manatee squeaking like a mouse underwater. I smile now, remembering how the manatee popped its eyes when I screamed.

I am Selkie, she'd said. My heart pounds as I realize something: I believe her.

43

Allie Jo

"We're not doing the brass today," I say when Chase meets me after his doctor's appointment. Brand-new cast, only D-A-D on it right now. I reach over the desk and grab the pink marker.

"No way!" he says, jerking his arm out of my reach.

I tip my head. "Come on," I say.

He makes a big show of resting his cast and hemming and hawing as I sign it. "What's it say?" he asks as I'm still writing.

"Cinnamon, aluminum, linoleum." And then, in little letters, I scribble my initials.

He frowns, trying to figure it out. "What does that mean?"

"Just read it."

So I listen to him read it three times in a row; each

time, he can't even get to the third word without sounding like he's underwater. I snicker at him.

This morning has been so busy with festival chores, I haven't had time to make my rounds; I haven't been able to look for Tara.

She said she was Selkie. Before yesterday, I'd never even heard of Selkies.

And Chase, he was so quiet and still when he came out of the springs last night. *That was incredible*, he'd said, his voice hushed and reverent. He wanted me to swim with Tara too, but I reminded him of all the trouble I got into swimming at night the last time. That's what I told him anyway. I felt safe with Tara in the garden room and on the grounds, but the darkness of the water and the closeness of the manatees were too scary for me. I did not want to do that again, not even with Tara.

A shiver goes through me right now just thinking about it.

I cap the pink marker and lay it on the desk. I'm about to ask Chase if he saw Tara before his doctor's visit, when Sophie arrives and makes a big deal about his new cast, signing in green this time. The circle over her *i* is shaped like a heart. I'll have to ask her about this later.

"Well!" Mom comes out of the office with Nicholas and Ryan. "All three of you! Where've you been hiding?"

Sophie and Chase laugh, but I know Mom means it.

After I came in from the springs last night, she grilled me good. She wanted to know what was wrong. *You look like you've seen a ghost,* she said, putting her hand on my forehead.

I'm okay, I said, pushing her hand away.

A look of hurt flashed across her face and she stepped back. Somewhere inside, I felt a pang of guilt and then a flicker of annoyance, which made me feel even guiltier. I wished they wouldn't pay so much attention to me sometimes. Things were coming up now that I had to think on, things I couldn't talk to them about, like Tara.

I hadn't seen a ghost—I'd seen a real, live Selkie.

Mom went into the kitchen and came back with a plate of cookies—every mom's cure—but I said I wasn't feeling well after all and slipped into my room, shutting the door. I needed to be alone.

If she was hurt, she feels better now, having me and everyone else buzzing around for the festival.

"Let's head into the workroom," Mom says. She tugs the third book on the third shelf of the bookcase under the grand staircase, and a portion of the wall creaks inward.

"Awesome!" Chase says.

We slip in, all of us, and walk under the rise of the stairs and enter what used to be a private screening room—a hidden theater for the rich and famous.

Of course, it doesn't look anything like it used to. The

room was gutted when the military was here. Instead of plush leather seats and a screen, the room now holds metal folding chairs and a few card tables. We mainly use it as a workroom.

Today, we're putting together wedding-type favors to pass out at Taste of Hope. Mom sets us up assembly line style: Chase puts candy wrapped with an embossed image of The Meriwether on top of lacy pink squares, which he pushes down to Sophie and me. Sophie and I pull up the corners and tie each little bundle with a fancy ribbon.

Some of last year's magnets are sticky with dust, so I give Nicholas and Ryan that job. They like spraying the cleaner on the magnets; I remind them they also have to dry them. That's why Ryan and Nicholas kneel on the floor, rubbing the magnets like crazy. I've promised each of them a dollar and a lollipop if they do a good job.

Sophie's fingers fly with the ribbon. Me, I'm all thumbs, and Chase isn't moving so fast with that cast either.

"Can I give you a *hand*?" I ask.

"Har, har," he says.

Sophie's going for some kind of world record. She doesn't talk, just whips the ribbons around and goes for the next one. She's building up a sizable arsenal of favors.

Clearing my throat, I say, "Um, Chase. Did you see any

cows today?" I'm talking in code because Sophie's sitting right with us.

His eyebrows wrinkle together. "What?"

I repeat, "Did you *see* any *cows* today?"

"No, just some roadkill." He's talking about his trip to the doctor's.

"Allie Jo!" Nicholas whines. "He got polish on my shoes."

Before I can say anything, he aims his bottle and sprays Ryan's shoes. Ryan starts bawling.

"That wasn't nice," I say, and frown at Nicholas. I take a dry paper towel and wipe off Ryan's shoes.

"He did it first," Nicholas says.

"No!" Ryan lunges at him. "It was an accident."

Nicholas shakes his head at him. "You're just a cry-baby brat!"

"Stop it, you guys!" I'm sitting between them because I know the hitting comes next. "Look, if you keep fighting, I won't give you lollipops." I stand up, reach over to the card table, and wave the lollipops in front of them. "Root beer, your favorite."

And just like that, they're friends again.

I wonder if it's always that easy with a brother or sister.

Sitting back down, I pick up the next bundle and fumble with the ribbon. "Nicholas, can you *tear a*"—I look straight at Chase—"piece of paper towel, please?"

Everyone keeps working. Nicholas hands me a paper towel and I wipe off an imaginary spot on the table.

Okay, this is ridiculous. Chase would never make a good spy. He doesn't even pick up on the code.

I give it one more try. "Sophie, can you *seal* this ribbon for me? *Seal* it?" I'm looking directly at Chase.

He slouches back in his seat. "Oh!"

"What?" Sophie asks, tying up my ribbon.

Chase and I speak at the same time. I say, "Nothing," and he says, "No, I didn't *see* any *cows* today."

Sophie crinkles her mouth. "You guys are weird."

Ryan pops up. "We're done!"

"Lollipops, please!" Nicholas says. Funny how candy is more important than money, but I'll still pay them.

Nicholas tears his lollipop open and hands me the plastic. Ryan hands his lollipop to Nicholas without saying a word; Nicholas opens it, gives me the plastic, and hands it back to Ryan. Then he pulls two little cars out of his pocket, and they roll the cars around the lobby, making sound effects.

It must be great having a brother. Of course, it'd be a sister I'd want, a built-in person to talk with. An older sister, who would give me advice on how to deal with boys and stuck-up girls. A girl who likes blueberry pancakes.

44

Chase

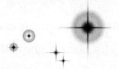

"Cool, awesome, excellent." I lean back on the beanbag and pet Jinx. "Tubular, gnarly—"

"Only boys use those words." Allie Jo turns to Tara. "*Cool, awesome,* and *excellent* for when you like something, and then, like, *totally cool* when something is very cool. *Gross* when something is disgusting."

We're giving Tara Selkie-to-English lessons. It's not like she doesn't already speak good English; it's just that her English is *too* good. She doesn't sound like a normal teenager.

"Listen." Allie Jo clicks on the tape recorder—we already explained how it works—and that same little girl I heard before is talking to an older girl. Allie Jo tells us the older girl is sixteen.

"If you weren't my sister, would you still be my friend?" The sound is muffled, like maybe the microphone is hidden under a pillow or something.

"Hmm," the older sister says. "You mean like if we were just neighbors or something?"

"Yeah, like if you were sitting on your porch and I rode my bike past you."

"Then I'd yell, 'Hey, you! Get off my yard!' "

The little girl clicks her tongue. "Karen."

There's the rustle of movement and Karen's voice is closer. "Of course I'd be your friend, silly. You're smart and funny, and you have freckles just like mine."

"Could I come over to your house sometimes?"

"Isabelle!" More movement. Karen's voice is farther away. "David's going to call in a minute."

The microphone crackles; then Isabelle's voice sounds close and whispery. "That's her boyfriend. She kisses him."

Allie Jo giggles at that part. I feel a faint blush heating my face.

"Now she sings some songs," Allie Jo says. "Let me get to more parts with Karen."

"Yes," Tara says. "I would like to hear Karen. I have a lot to learn if I'm going to live here."

"Here?" Allie Jo blurts out. "You mean, like, The Meriwether?"

Jinx climbs onto Tara's shoulders and Tara leans her head into the cat. Smiling, she says, "This is a good place to be human."

Allie Jo shoots up like fireworks. "You could stay in this room!" she says, exploding in sparkles.

"With the jinx?" Tara asks, absently reaching up to pet the cat.

Oh, man, she seriously needs the Selkie-to-English lesson plan.

I explain. "Jinx is her *name*—she's a cat!" Then I have a great idea. "If you're going to live here, we should create a new identity for you, like they do for people in the witness protection program."

Allie Jo contorts her face. "Why?"

"Just in case."

Tara shakes her head. "I feel safe here. But"—she looks at Allie Jo—"a human identity would be good. Where do we start?"

"With a full name." I've watched plenty of detective shows, and this is how criminals always get away: they use a new name, they change their looks, and they move to a different part of the country. So far, Tara's done one of those things. "And we have to make you look different."

So that's how we end up in my room, with a pair of scissors and a box of Summer Blonde hair dye that Allie Jo snuck out of her mom's bathroom. I watch from the doorway as Allie Jo blow-dries Tara's new hair.

Though it's kind of choppy, I say, "It looks good."

Tara's hand flies up to the short ends of her hair. "Thank you," she says. She stares into the bathroom mirror, stunned. I'm not sure, but I think I see tears in her eyes.

I glance at the long, dark hair on the floor. "Do you miss being a Selkie?"

She closes her eyes.

"Are you kidding?" Allie Jo says. "We're going to have so much fun!" She hugs Tara's shoulders and looks at her in the mirror. "First, you're going to help with Taste of Hope, which you'll get paid for because you're my employee, and then you can start school—what grade will you be in, eleventh, I think. And—oh, my gosh!—I could ask Dad to give you a real job here and we'll do everything together and it will be great, right?" She nudges Tara.

Tara opens her eyes and looks at Allie Jo in the mirror. "Totally."

Allie Jo nods with approval. "See? You're already getting it!"

As Allie Jo busies herself with cleaning up the hair and the sink, I lean my head against the door frame and close my eyes. Images crash through my mind in waves. The dark swirl of the springs underwater at night; me, holding on tightly as Tara glided through the rushing current, propelled by the powerful motion of her arms; her hair, flowing in the water as though wind blew through it.

I remember how Tara looked when she emerged from the springs. *As one truly born again, her face shone with joy unsurpassed, the beautiful mystery of which she was a part. Even the moon baptized her with its glory.*

The water is her home. She won't survive without it.

45

Allie Jo

We decide to take Tara out for a field trip. Our first stop is the front desk. A bunch of people wait in line; the crowd for Taste of Hope is starting to fill the hotel. More people come in and wait behind us. We even had to walk single file down the hallway to make way for people and their suitcases. This is my absolute favorite time of year.

When we finally get up to the front, I'm about to say, *Hay, Clay,* but his eyes boing out of his head when he sees Tara.

Time for witness protection. "Clay, this is Tara . . . Blume," I say, giving her the last name of one of my favorite authors. "She's Melanie's cousin." The cousin part was something I thought of while I was dyeing Tara's hair. I would love to say she's *my* cousin, but Clay would know that wasn't true.

"Nice to meet you," Tara says, and smiles. So far, she is getting an A-plus.

Clay's face turns red.

"Clay?" Boy, I tell you, liking someone can really turn people into dorks.

"Hi, Allie Jo," he says without turning from Tara.

I ding the bell a whole bunch of times and say, "Uh . . . I'm over here."

Shock takes over Clay's face and it gets even redder.

"Tell Dad we're going downtown."

He nods.

"Nice to meet you," Tara says again, and we head outside, where Chase is waiting for us.

Armed with Taste of Hope posters, hammers, and nails, our job is to replace any posters that have fallen off telephone poles or have been ruined by rain. That's why we walk downtown; besides, the shuttle bus was loaded with people heading out to the boutiques.

The first poster has been rained on so much, all the colors have run. I yank it off the post. "Throw this in the trash can over there," I direct Chase.

Holding a new one in its place, I grab a nail and hit it with the hammer, but the wood's hard.

"Let me," Tara says. With one powerful thwack, she drives the nail in. Her hair looks a little uneven. I make a mental note to fix that when we get home.

We trudge down the road looking for other signs. By the time we get onto the main strip, we've replaced seventeen posters; looking down the street, I can see at least seventeen more.

You can tell by all the cars cruising the boulevard that the festival is kicking up. Joanie's Closet is having a sidewalk sale; that's where I get most of my clothes. Farther down, people come in and out of Fine Exotics by Sima carrying their purchases in the special silver bags she gives out. I see Miss MaryAnn sitting outside her studio painting; she wears a beret and looks like a real artist, which I guess she is, since she's from New York.

Waiting at the stoplight is pure torture. I roast like a peanut. Tara's face is red, and Chase is scratching his cast. A crowd of people cluster on the other side. Finally, a rooster crows, signaling it's okay for us to cross. Hope Springs doesn't just have a *Walk/Don't Walk* sign; we have a rooster noise hooked up to the light. It's just another one of those things that makes this place special.

As we cross, a couple of people pretend not to look at Tara, but they can't help it. She's so pretty.

I just know she's going to be popular in school, but unlike most popular people, she'll be nice, which will make her even more popular. Sure, she'll have other friends, but I'll be the one she's closest to, because she *picked* me. We'll sit on the porch and do our homework together.

I glance at her, and she smiles back at me. This fall is going to be the best school year ever.

Heat rolls up from the blacktop, and I look at all those signs lining the street. Sweat trickles down my back under my shirt. "Let's go to Brimble's," I say.

We sit out on the porch, knocking back our lemonades.

Chase leans forward on his rocker. "There's your friend," he says out of the side of his mouth.

Jennifer Jorgensen! Does she have to be everywhere? "Don't even look at her," I say, and stare straight ahead. But I'm keeping the side of my eyes on her.

Of course she's not alone—Heather and Lori are with her, and of course they can't just pass by; they come straight up the steps. They don't even have the decency to pretend they don't see us.

Jennifer walks over and squares herself against the banister right in front of Chase. My eyes turn into slits. The other girls don't quite know what to do with themselves because Jennifer's blocking the way.

"Hi, Chase," she says, trying to make her dimples show. She glances right through me and startles at Tara. Then she straightens up. "Who are you?"

"Tara," she says. "I'm Melanie's cousin."

Jennifer screws up her face, turning her nostrils into a pig nose. "You're Melanie's cousin?"

"And Allie Jo's friend."

She's sticking up for me. My chest swells with emotion. This is what it's like; this is what it's like to have a sister.

Tara stands up, causing Jennifer to look up at her. "What's your name?" Tara asks.

Jennifer's face tightens. She looks a little scared. "Jennifer," she says.

Lori pushes forward a little. "I'm Lori and this is Heather. Are you a model?"

"Omigosh!" Heather chimes in. "I was just about to ask the same thing!"

They chat Tara up as Jennifer takes her in. Then Jennifer ducks out behind them and kneels by Chase's rocking chair.

"Can I sign your cast?"

He shrugs. "If you want to."

She pops up and claps her hands. They crowd into the shop and Jennifer comes back lickety-split to Chase's side with a marker. She scans his cast, looking for just the right spot when her eyes land on something that stops her flat. "Oh—*Sophie*."

With a green heart, like Jennifer's is right now.

She scribbles her trademark signature, a big *J* followed by smaller letters in the bowl of the *J*. So really, if you had to pronounce it, you'd have to say *Enniferj*.

After she goes back into Brimble's, I get up. "Let's finish these signs," I say. And get far away from Enniferj.

46

Chase

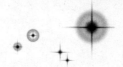

"I didn't want her to sign it," I say to Allie Jo as we head up the road. "I just didn't know how I could say no."

"I know," she says.

Tara goes, "It's cool."

I look at Tara and laugh. "Excellent!" Man, she's quick.

The sun blasts us as we work our way up the street, pounding in the new signs. We have two left; they're on wickets and we're supposed to stick them in the park where Taste of Hope will be.

Allie Jo tugs the back of my shirt. "Let's go in here first."

Joanie's Closet. Oh, no. I sag, my arms drooping like a toy robot that's run out of batteries. I hate shopping. My aunt forces me to go with her sometimes. I'd rather scrub toilets with my toothbrush than look at clothes.

"C'mon," Allie Jo says. "It'll only take a minute."

I groan. That's what they all say.

Joanie's Closet smells like a basement, musty but good. There is no way I'm looking at clothes, so I kind of wander around and find myself at a jewelry counter.

I take a mood ring from on top of a basket of loose jewelry and put it on.

A lady steps up behind the counter. "What mood are you in?"

I watch the ring as the blackness dissolves into swirls of color. "I don't know," I say.

She looks down at the ring through her bifocals, then pulls out a chart. "Violet," she says, running her finger across the card. She looks up at me and smiles. "You're feeling happy and romantic."

"Cheeyah." I jerk the ring off my finger and drop it into the basket. "Those things don't really work. They just measure your temperature, that's all."

"Not true," she says. I wonder if she's Joanie. "It's all scientific." She snugs the ring onto her own finger, waits a minute, then says, "See? Blue. I'm relaxed and lovable." She grins.

I sort through the jewelry and spot a glimmer of green near the bottom. Fishing through all the chains and stuff, I hook the band and pull out a silver ring with a shiny, light green stone shaped like a heart.

Sophie! This will make it official.

"Happy and romantic," the lady says as she rings me up.

I don't want Allie Jo and Tara to see it, so I shove it into my pocket and tell them I'll wait outside for them. When they finally come out, they sit on a bench and pull out everything they just bought and admire it. Now this is something I don't understand: Didn't they just spend twenty minutes looking at that stuff? Did they already forget what it looks like? They laugh and giggle, telling each other how good the other will look in this or that shirt. I shake my head. They're just like my aunt.

I look across to the hilly park, where vendors have parked their trailers and begun to set up.

"Hey, there's my dad!" I say.

We cross over, shoving the wicket signs in as we climb the slight hill. Cords lie all over the grass, snaking to their owner's tents. Not all the tents are built yet; some have only the framework up, and some spots have the equipment dumped in a heap. It looks like a battle encampment.

"That's good," Dad says, scribbling down the thing about a battle encampment. "Mind if I use it?"

"Don't forget my percentage," I say. Onlookers mill around, dodging wires and poles. The smell of cut grass wafts in the air.

"Hi, Mr. Dennison," Allie Jo says after she and Tara catch up to me. She introduces Tara, then asks, "You getting stuff for your article?"

Dad shakes his head in wonder. "This town went from dead to population explosion overnight. It's incredible!"

"Almost two hundred thousand people are expected," Allie Jo says. She talks like a guidebook. "That's ten times more than the number of people who live here."

Dad scribbles that in his notebook.

"Just for fireworks?" I can't believe that.

"Not just fireworks," Allie Jo says. She gestures toward the tents. "There'll be painters, street entertainers, food and hospitality booths—this is, like, one of the biggest festivals in Florida." She looks at Dad. "Did you get all that down?"

He laughs. "Yes, I did."

She leans over and puts her finger on Dad's notebook. "Could you put that The Meriwether will be serving five-star food, including blueberry pancakes and shrimp cocktail?"

Pancakes with shrimp. "That's gross!" I say.

"Not together!" She turns to Dad. "Chef will turn the menu over for lunch and dinner."

Tara runs her hand over her hair, looks from me to Allie Jo. "I need to go." Sweat rolls down the side of her face.

Allie Jo points to the portable toilets. "Let's go."

Tara's pupils widen. When she looks at me, I feel pinpricks of heat.

"I don't think that's what she means," I say to Allie Jo, watching Tara warily. Something's wrong, only I can't ask in front of Dad. "Can I have my percentage now?" I ask him. "We're too fried to walk back."

He gives me bus fare for all of us and says he'll meet me at the hotel later. Tara walks so briskly to the bus stop that I think we might have gotten back faster just by keeping up with her. But the bus comes around quickly and the air-conditioning chills me as soon as we step on.

I settle in the back with them, slouching in my seat. Finally out of that heat.

Tara's taken the window, leaning forward just enough to see out. Her back is straight and her hands are clasped in a knot on her lap.

Even though the air-conditioning blows directly on me, the heat pinpricks bristle from my face to my legs. Man, there's no escape from it.

47

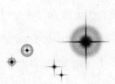

Safe.

Sitting with her back against the wall and Jinx brushing against her legs, Tara felt relief flooding through her limbs. She was glad to be away from the crowd of humans. So many of them. Their currents mixed and crossed over each other, roiling through the air with the rising heat. Allie Jo seemed to enjoy this chaos; for Tara, it caused only vexation.

The feeling had crept over her as they entered the downtown area. Not that silly girl, Jennifer; the age of being was coming over her. Tara could sense Jennifer's blood, hot and rushing. She would have to tell Allie Jo this—the girl was nothing for Allie Jo to worry about.

A slight breeze wandered through the room, carrying the sweet fragrance of the white flowered trees in the lawns below—magnolias, Allie Jo had told her. Their perfume was lovely and intoxicating.

Sighing, she glanced up at the bud partially enclosed by kudzu leaves. She'd thought it to be some kind of wart when she noticed it a few days ago, but now she saw that it had changed. She touched it and something beat against her fingers. Life grew inside! How odd and amazing.

She wondered if she would ever grow accustomed to life on land.

When the bus had returned them to the hotel, people streamed in, like fish going downstream. Chase asked her what was wrong, but she couldn't explain; she herself was too perplexed.

Men and women bumped into her, some looking back to say excuse me, others moving on slowly, like sea cows.

She felt confused, lost—too many sensations. Following Allie Jo's lead, she had taken a seat in the Emerald Dining Room and they had lunch with Allie Jo's mother.

"This spinach is quite good," Tara had said. She ate something called a salad. "Like kudzu," she added.

A brief look of confusion crossed Mrs. Jackson's face. Then Allie Jo started laughing. "You are so funny," she said, but her eyes carried a warning.

Tara longed for this lunch to be over. Mrs. Jackson asked many questions: "Where are you from?" "How's Melanie doing?" and even worse, "Your mom and dad let you come by yourself?"

Tara guarded her words, lest she become ensnared. Still, the woman seemed delighted when Allie Jo announced that Tara helped with the signs and would continue to help throughout the festival.

"It's a madhouse," Mrs. Jackson declared, yet the face she wore was one of glee.

Tara despaired of ever truly understanding humans.

Today had been very hot, hot enough to make sweat come out of her skin. Yet she'd had pleasure in being outside and in receiving the new clothes Allie got her. One was a bathing suit, stretchy with skinny straps. Such flimsy skin would never work in the seas, but here in the springs, it would be perfect.

Tomorrow, they would help Chef arrange platters. Shrimp cocktail. Tomorrow would be good. She could hardly wait.

For now, she was drained. She closed her eyes and snuggled into the beanbag, pulling Jinx onto her lap. Jinx purred, soft tendrils of sound that encircled her like a warm, rolling fog. It was not long before sleep took them both.

48

Allie Jo

I tap my clipboard like Dad does and read my assignments out loud. "Chase and boys: brass. Sophie, Tara, and I: kitchen duty."

"No fair," Chase says, groaning. "You guys are just going to be eating."

Clutching my clipboard, I go, "It's a proven fact girls have more sensitive taste buds than boys." I read that somewhere, so you know it's true. Besides, "Tara's a seafood expert."

We've gathered in the front parlor to divide the tasks. I snuck out one of the front-desk jackets so everyone would know I was official. And they do too, because I see some of them glance at me and smile. "Welcome to The Meriwether," I say to their smiles.

"That's another thing," I remind my employees. "Always be friendly to the guests. Even if they put their hands all over your just-polished rails, you just smile and wait till they're gone and do it again. Remember, the customer is always right."

Nicholas throws his rag to the ground. "I don't want to do this."

"You have to," I say. "I'm babysitting you right now."

Chase grins. "Actually, I'll be babysitting them right now, so . . ."

I tighten my lips and put a mark by his name. Supervising is hard work. "I'll be back to check on you."

Chase salutes me and snaps his feet together. Nicholas and Ryan laugh, then copy him.

Tara, Sophie, and I slowly work our way down the crowded hall. I know the customer is always right, but would it kill them to move over a little? I lead the way in my Meriwether jacket.

Sophie had been surprised to see Tara at the parlor. She whispered in my ear, "Who's that?"

I'd spent so much time with Tara I clean forgot not everybody had met her. "This is Tara, Melanie's cousin."

Tara bent a little. "Nice to meet you." I smiled proudly at my student.

"Sophie's teaching me to knit." My scarf was longer

than a ruler now. I'd already put it up against my favorite
shirts to see what looked most fashionable with it.

Tara said, "Oh," and I realized they probably didn't
knit underwater.

Now in the dining room, I push on the swinging door
and see the kitchen is as busy as an ant colony. Cooks in
white uniforms—I don't know why they wear white; they
should wear shirts with splotched-up colors so they never
look dirty—glide across the floor with trays and some work
over the grills. The walk-in refrigerator needs a revolving
door for all the traffic.

"Allie Jo!" Chef calls out. He glances at my clipboard
and my jacket and pulls his fuzzy eyebrows together under
his hat. "You're not here to inspect, are you?"

I laugh and introduce him to Tara and Sophie.

He nods. "A committee, huh? Go around then, I'll meet
you in the break room."

Even though I do so much work around here, I'm not
technically considered an employee, so Chef doesn't like
me to walk through the kitchen for insurance reasons.
We walk around into the hallway and slip through an
unmarked door.

"Ooh," Tara says, looking at the shrimp cocktail.

Chef has outdone himself. Seven peach-colored shrimp
curve over the rim of a martini glass. Thin ribbons of yellow squash and green cucumber cascade over the side, and

he's drawn a zigzag in cocktail sauce across the plate. It looks like a present.

We sit at the table and I shove the shrimp over to Tara. "You first."

Lifting one from the glass, she giggles. "No shell!"

"Of course not!" Chef says. "I peel them."

Tara crunches into one and savors that bit for so long, I get impatient. "Well—how is it?"

Tara closes her eyes and smiles. Chef puts his hand on my shoulder and says, "We're in the presence of a gourmet, not a gourmand like you." By that he means Tara likes fine food, while I just like a lot of food.

It hits me then that Chef would probably hire Tara. My plan is working out well.

"You're right," I say. "Where are my pancakes?"

He takes the cover off a buffet pan and serves Sophie and me blueberry pancakes, silver dollar size. They look like cookies. I pick one up with my fingers and eat it whole. "Excellent," I say with my mouth full. "Doesn't even need syrup."

Sophie laughs shyly and picks up a fork.

Tara makes nice little comments to Sophie and Chef, and everyone likes her. I'm so happy. She fits right in. In fact, I don't see why she has to hide upstairs—when the festival is over, we'll have plenty of extra rooms. I'm sure Dad would give her one.

Or—and my heart practically bursts with joy when I think this—she could stay at my house! My room is plenty big enough, and I don't mind using a sleeping bag on the floor. Mom and Dad would get so used to her, they wouldn't even want her to move out. Maybe they would adopt her!

I plow through the pancakes, I'm so excited.

A sister. A sister! Every night, we'll stay up late talking. Probably she'll go out on dates and I'll be all mad because she used my nail polish or perfume or something, but then, when she comes back, we'll lie on our beds and she'll tell me everything. She'll tell me who she went out with and what movie they saw and if they kissed at the end of the night. Our secrets will come out in the darkness.

"Slow down, Allie Jo!" Chef says. "Slow down!"

I laugh. "I can't! Everything is too good." And I mean it when I say, "This is going to be the best Taste of Hope ever!"

☾

The committee is doing pretty well eating, so I decide to check on Chase and the boys. Good thing too, because when I get there, all three of them are leaning against the wall.

Chase gestures with a rag before I can say anything.

"It's that guy," he says. "He's keeps talking with Clay and your dad, and he's all over the brass."

Probably looking for a room or something. Too bad. We're full up. I wander closer in to overhear the problem.

"Allie Jo," Dad says. His face is very serious. Quickly, I review my day and decide I haven't done anything wrong.

I step up to the desk, careful not to put my shoe on the footrail in case it's already been polished. Unlike *some* people, I think, looking down at the man's sneakers.

"This man, Mr.— Uh, what was your name, sir?"

"Mr. Smith." His voice is flat.

Dad turns to me. "Mr. Smith here is looking for his niece. She was staying with him but—"

"She ran away." The man turns his watery eyes to me. They're cracked with red lines. "She . . . has some problems." His eyes droop; his shoulders sag; everything about him is pulled down.

He flashes a picture. "Have you seen her?"

Fire alarms ring in my ears. My mouth drops open and my eyes pop out. It's Tara, inside a messy living room. Beer cans and peanut shells litter the room; the TV's on, but she's not watching it. She's staring into the camera like a wild animal. My breath comes out in short bursts.

His eyes focus. "You've seen her."

"No." My heart bangs so loud I'm sure he can hear it. But I'm not ready to say yes. I stare at the picture. It's Tara, all right, and she's got on the same outfit I first saw her in. "I've never seen her," I say.

My heart hammers and I turn away, but he grips my wrist. "Are you sure?" He slants his eyes. "It looked like you recognized her."

"Let go of my daughter," Dad orders. He comes around and inserts himself between me and Mr. Smith.

"I'm sorry, I'm sorry," Mr. Smith says, lifting his palms up. Then he raises glum eyes to Dad. "I'm sure as a father you can understand how upsetting this can be. She's been with me since her parents died." He presses his palms against his eyes. "Pamela's very special to me, but she's not quite right in the head. She lives in a fantasy world. I'm afraid someone could hurt her."

"Have you tried the police?" Dad asks. He leans over the counter, pulls up the phone, and is about to dial when Mr. Smith shakes his head and waves his hands.

"Police, private detective, shelters—everything. They haven't found her. That's why I'm out here on my own." He swipes another look at me. "But if she's not here, she's not here." His shoulders slump and he heads toward the front door.

Thoughts dart in my head like tadpoles in the water. I feel all hurly-burly. Maybe I should run after that man and tell him what I know. I don't know what to do. My eyes well up.

Dad puts his arm around my shoulders. "Are you okay? It looks like he scared the heck out of you."

I turn my face into the crook of Dad's arms, and big, fat tears roll down my face. I know he's got to get back to the guests, but I need him right now. After a minute or so goes by, I mumble into his chest, "I'm okay."

He holds me by the shoulders and looks at me. "Are you sure?"

I nod and smile. It's always the smile that convinces them.

After he returns behind the desk, Chase rushes over. "What's the deal?" he asks in a low voice. He lasers in on me.

I wipe my nose with the back of my hand and sniffle.

"Did you get in trouble again?" He's talking very gently, like you would to a cat you were trying to get out from under a bush.

Dazed, I turn past him, walk around the grand staircase to the parlor, and drop onto a couch. Nicholas, Ryan, and Chase follow me.

"You guys play cars," I say. Like magicians, they produce cars from their pockets and race them along the banister.

Chase sits beside me. "What's wrong?" he asks again.

I turn to him in a trance. "That was Tara's uncle."

His face contorts. "What?"

"He said her name is Pamela and that her parents died, which is why she lives with him, and she's sort of . . . sort of . . ."

He leans in. "Sort of what?"

My eyebrows pucker and the corners of my lips turn down. "She's sort of crazy."

49

Chase

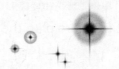

"Crazy?" I breathe like I just ran five laps. "What did he say?"

She tells me the whole thing, how sad the man looked, and that he was worried someone would hurt Tara—Pamela—because she lived in a fantasy world.

"He said she's not quite right in the head." Allie Jo's eyes ask me to agree or disagree, but I'm still reeling from the word *crazy*.

I take a deep breath and close my eyes, shut out the hotel and all these people and even Allie Jo.

"Chase?" She nudges me in the ribs. "It makes more sense, right?"

I bow my head. "Yeah . . . it makes more sense." I mean, a seal that can turn into a human? My heart falls into my stomach. She'd made it seem so real, with the moonlight swimming and calling to manatees. And how she likes fish, and how she talks, and even her long, dark hair that dangled almost to her waist like seaweed. I press my fist to my chest; there's that pain again.

Oh, man. Why couldn't there be one cool thing this summer? But the knot in my chest unravels when I remember Sophie. The green heart ring is upstairs on my nightstand. I'm just trying to plan the right time to give it to her.

For now, though, I've gotta find out what's going on with Tara. "Come on," I say to Allie Jo. "Let me do the talking."

When we knock on the door of the employee break room, Chef ushers us in with the boys. "More testers!" Chef says. "I have no more shrimp, no more pancakes!" He looks at Nicholas and Ryan. "But I do have chocolate chip cookies!"

That's all they need to hear. They follow him to the door of the kitchen; Allie Jo and I sit at a table with Tara and Sophie.

"So," I say to Allie Jo. "Maybe you should get an extra cookie for *Pamela*." I'm expecting a knee jerk, a gasp, or something from Tara, but her expression stays the same.

"Yes," Allie Jo says. "I'm sorry her parents died. I wish she would've told me."

Someone does gasp, but it's Sophie. She asks Allie Jo,

"You have a friend whose parents died?" Her eyes widen. "That's terrible."

"She doesn't want anyone to know," I say.

"She's pretending it didn't happen," Allie Jo adds.

Sophie breathes out a quiet *Wow.* We all sit there, silent, thinking.

"Cookies!" Nicholas and Ryan come running back in. Ryan eats by smashing the cookie into his mouth.

Tara runs a hand over her hair. I can tell she wishes Allie Jo hadn't dyed and cut it.

She looks straight at me, her eyes deep and endless. Chills crawl up my spine and the hairs on the back of my neck stand up.

Pamela or Tara?

We can't ask her right out because of the boys and Sophie, or maybe that's a secret we don't need to keep anymore. But it doesn't seem like a good idea to bust out with the news. If she does have something wrong with her, it might send her off into the deep end.

I want to find out more from Allie Jo, but the only second I'm alone with her is at the sink, when I pretend I need to wash my hands.

"I don't think her name's Pamela," I say under my breath.

"Why would he lie about her name?" she asks.

Then everyone's at the sink, washing their hands,

getting ready for the next task. Allie Jo still has to babysit the boys, and I don't want to leave Sophie, so the afternoon turns into evening with all of us working for Taste of Hope.

I'm actually bushed after Dad and I get back to our room after supper. He flips through his notes and turns on the typewriter.

"You get a lot of stuff for your article?" I ask.

"Oh, yeah," he says. "Lots of good photos too." Then he turns, leaning one arm over the back of his chair. "I saw manatees in the springs today—manatees!"

My ears prick up, but I shrug to act casual.

"Usually you only see them here in the winter," he explains. "But I took a whole roll of film on them."

I hesitate before replying. "That's kind of strange, isn't it?"

Dad's face breaks into a big smile. "Yes! The photos are going to be incredible." He describes the manatees to me, their walrus shape, the way they float through the water, big yet graceful.

Yeah, I know, I want to say. *I swam with one.* He has no idea.

"Dad, remember last year when they discovered that giant squid?" With tentacles almost fifty feet long, the squid made all the papers.

"Yeah?" He's loading the typewriter with a piece of

paper, not really listening now. That's okay, because I don't want what I'm about to say to seem important.

"Well, before that, people just thought it was a legend, right? Like something out of *Twenty Thousand Leagues Under the Sea*?"

"Guess Jules Verne knew what he was talking about." Dad starts pecking. For a guy who uses only two fingers, he's pretty fast.

"Do you think there's other stuff like that, stuff that could be true?"

Tap, tap. "Sure, why not? We've got men flying through space, black holes in the universe, and supernovas—who knows what they'll discover next."

"I mean more like legends. You know, Loch Ness monster, Bigfoot—"

He chuckles. "I want the first scoop on those stories."

I think of more legends. "Trolls . . . mermaids . . . Selkies—"

Dad spins around in his chair. His gaze is open but penetrating. "Why are you asking me this stuff?"

I mask my face really quick. "No reason. Just . . . you were talking about the manatees and that made me think of the squid, that's all."

He stares at me for a moment, a moment I have to get out of. He looks like maybe he thinks I'm nuts.

I pick up the remote, settle on a game show, and pretend to be absorbed.

After a few minutes, the pecking starts up again. *Clack, clack, clack. Clack, clack, clack. Clackety-clack, clack, clack. Ding! Clack, clack.* Then the carriage return zips back to the left margin.

If Tara's crazy, we need to find her uncle. But if she's *not* crazy . . .

Clack, clack, clack. Clack, clack, clack. Clackety-clack, clack, clack.

50

Allie Jo

When I see Sophie at breakfast the next day, she looks positively terrible. Her eyes float in their sockets; her nose runs; even her hair looks sick.

"Don't sit too close!" Mrs. Duran says. "Sophie's got a cold."

Sophie sneezes five times in a row as if to prove it. My own sneezes come in sets of two.

I sit in a chair across the table from Sophie, the one Mrs. Duran has pulled out. My science teacher told us last year that the air and moisture, by which he means spit, from an average sneeze travels at around sixty miles per hour.

Sophie starts to say hi but sneezes again. I'm sure one of them was a direct hit—these tables are only four feet across.

"Hi, Sophie."

"Hi." Her voice sounds gunked up and plugged. The only time I like to be that way is during the school year.

Mrs. Duran rises from her seat. "I'm going to use the restroom. Be right back."

Sophie wads up some tissue to her nose and blurts into it.

"You don't sound too good," I say.

"I don't feel so good either," she says, except her *don't* sounds like *dode*. "Um . . . ," she starts.

"Yeah?"

"I was wondering, like, um . . ." She shrugs one shoulder, laughs at herself, then looks away before looking back at me. "You and Chase—"

"What?" It comes so fast out of my mouth that I almost hit her with it. "What about me and Chase?"

"The way you guys were talking yesterday . . ."

"Yeah?"

"And how you guys hang out a lot . . ."

Oh, my gosh—does she know? My face tenses. "Yeah, yeah?"

"Well . . . what I mean is"—she curls up on her chair and leans forward—"do you guys . . . like each other?"

I almost fall out of my seat, half laughing, half relieved.

She looks confused. "It's okay if you do, you know."

"NO! I don't *like* like Chase!" I give a little shudder. Puh-leeze!

She brightens. "Really?"

"Really!"

She sighs. "Thanks, Allie Jo."

Then she sneezes big-time; I count seven in a row. Yep, this would definitely be a free day out of school.

She's still snorkeling into her tissues when a voice comes up behind me.

"What a surprise," a man's voice says. As he comes around, I see it's Mr. Smith—Tara's uncle. He has a sour smell even though he's wearing different clothes. A Meriwether cup steams in his hand.

I jolt upright in my seat. "Are you a guest here?"

"Just here for breakfast," he says. Even though his eyes are still red and glazed, he hones in on me. He plants his coffee cup on our table and reaches into his shirt pocket. "Thought you might have had time to think about that picture I showed you."

Sophie shrinks back when he steps up between us and snaps down the picture of Tara in front of me. *I don't think her name's Pamela,* Chase had said.

Mr. Smith kneels to my height in the chair. "Remember, she needs help. I'm her only family." He spouts out the same words as yesterday, but it's like he's reciting them. Leaning closer, he mutters, "You've seen her."

My body revs up like a race car at the starting line.

His voice comes out rough. "Tell me." Then he takes a

big breath and blows it out. His eyes soften. His voice is gentler, but he speaks through clenched teeth. "Please. You *have* a father and a mother. She *lost* hers—that's why she's so mixed up." He licks his lips. "I need her back."

Heart pounding, I open my mouth. "I—I—"

"Excuse me!" Mrs. Duran calls out from the hostess stand. Her face is set like stone as she makes her way briskly toward the table. Her blue eyes are cold as ice.

Mr. Smith snatches up the picture, slides it into his shirt pocket, and presses his fingers into my shoulder. "Think about it." He scowls, leaving before Mrs. Duran reaches our table.

Mrs. Duran hurries over to us. "Do you know him?"

My resolve crumbles and tears fill my eyes.

Her face hardens. She turns after him. "Excuse me? Excuse me?" But he barrels into the hall and disappears among the guests.

"Are you all right?" She strokes my hair. "What did he say to you?"

Sophie sneezes a big one into a new wad of tissues. "He showed her a picture." She wipes her nose and stares at me. "Who is he?"

I shake my head. "I'm not sure," I say, and it's true. Reaching for one of Sophie's tissues, I try to ignore what my tears are telling me.

You have a father and a mother. She lost hers. How mixed

up would I be if Mom and Dad died? I rub my nose with the tissue. I can't think of a world without Mom and Dad in it. But I do, and more tears threaten to flood my face. Then I picture them losing me. They'd go to the ends of the earth to find me, just like Mr. Smith is doing for Tara.

Sniffling, I sit straight up and rub my eyes with my hands. I think I know what I should do now.

51

Chase

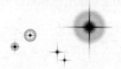

Allie Jo tells me I just missed Sophie. "And that's not all," she says. She fills me in on Mr. Smith showing up again.

I'm steaming hot. We're folding towels out by the pool cabinet. With so many guests here for the festival, the pool is finally getting some use. Only a few people brave the springs.

"He's not her uncle." The sun scorches the top of my head.

"How do *you* know?"

I shrug. "I just do."

Apparently, that's not a good enough answer, because then she goes, "Well, then, how would he know her and how would he have a picture of her?"

"If you think he's her uncle," I start, "why didn't you tell him she's here?"

Three kids link arms and leap into the water, splashing us. I don't flinch like Allie Jo does; the cold drops feel good.

She refolds my last towel. "I almost did." Sighing, she goes, "She said she's a runaway, and here he is looking for her. I mean, how would he even know? It doesn't make sense if he's not her uncle."

Still, something's not right here. "I got a bad feeling from him at the front desk."

The kids in the pool start playing Marco Polo. "Man, it's hot," I say. "Let's go sit by the springs."

We wrap up the last few towels and cross the lawn to the springs.

I crash on the concrete pad and dunk my feet in. "Aah!" *The boy's body longed to plunge into the frigid water, but he dared not, for the father would not like the new cast getting wet.* Still, I move to the edge and stick my legs in as far as they can go.

Allie Jo does the same. "But do you know what I mean? Why would he be looking for her if he wasn't her uncle? And how does he know her name?"

"Her name's *not* Pamela; she doesn't even notice that name." As proven by my experiment when Sophie and she were doing the taste tests.

"She doesn't notice it because maybe she *is* a little . . . not right in the head. Maybe she believes she's this whole other person. If she is . . . *off*, she needs her family." Allie Jo stirs her feet in the water, sending ripples my way. She hunches over. "People just can't turn into seals; that's not even possible."

I close my eyes and my mind goes underwater, shooting through the green and blue depths of the springs. I remember Tara's power and grace that night; I remember the moonbeams.

I am Selkie.

Allie Jo elbows me. "Chase, right? It's not even possible."

Glancing at her wordlessly, I turn back to the springs, shut my eyes, and slip away.

52

Allie Jo

I don't understand why I couldn't get Chase to agree with me about Tara yesterday. When I was little, I was a mermaid, a princess, a girl who could fly—I was lots of things and they were all make-believe, but I knew it.

Tara doesn't know it.

She really believes she's a Selkie. Even if there were such a thing, she would look more like one, like, like—I don't know—how vampires have fangs and fairies have wings. I tried to point this out to Chase but he didn't agree or disagree. It was so frustrating.

One thing I don't need anyone to instruct me on is family. If Tara's uncle hadn't shown up, she would have been part of *my* family. I was planning it, I could imagine it, and it wasn't make-believe either. It was real. But a blood

relative is even more real. I woke up this morning knowing that.

If I see Mr. Smith again, I'll reunite him with Tara—
Pamela. Family needs each other.

☾

Even though it's six fifteen in the morning, the hotel staff
buzzes with excitement. Everyone who's helping at Taste of
Hope sits in the break room as Dad gives out last-minute
instructions. The dark smell of coffee fills the room, and
the adults guzzle it to start their engines.

Sophie's parents left a note for me at the front desk
that Sophie had a fever last night and is too sick to come
out. I feel bad for her, but I'll get her some goodies from
the other booths.

Chase and Tara sit with me at a table in the back.
We've got fancy waitstaff uniforms on, and everyone looks
sharp. Glancing at Tara, I see her hair's wet, probably from
an early morning swim. My heart falls upon realizing this.
I try to raise a smile in her direction, but now I feel sad
thinking that something is not right in her brain.

I wonder if it's a person's fault if they're sick in the
head. Maybe they need to pay attention or read more
books. But I don't think so. I don't think it's their fault. On
TV, they show mental patients acting all weird, like having

a million different personalities or killing people. I don't think those TV people have ever met someone with brain problems. Tara's good. She would never do that stuff.

"Okay!" Dad claps his hands and we file out to the shuttle buses.

Clay leaves the front desk for a moment to walk with Tara, and Chase takes this opportunity to argue with me about her and her uncle. He wonders why her uncle doesn't call the police or offer a reward or something. He calls the man a creep, a schemer who wants to kidnap her.

I'm done talking about this. I shut him up by saying, "Or maybe he's just her uncle come to take care of her."

When we get to the park, Mrs. Brimble and her daughter in college, Toni, are washing down bistro tables on the lower end of the hill, where their booth is set up.

"Hey, Toni!" I yell. "Hi, Mrs. Brimble!" They straighten up, smile, and wave back.

I pass the booth for Books 'n' Such. "Hi, Miss Pauline!" I scan her booth real quick. Yep, she's got the jar where you drop your name in, and later you might be the winner of a free book of your choice. I'll be back here for sure. Gracie's Attic, Flowers & Vines by Sieg, Coffee Haus, Anne-tiques—they're all here. Miss Joanie is talking with Miss MaryAnn, who has already set up her easel and is painting on her first canvas of the day.

Looking up and down at the rows and rows of

tents and calling out to people, my heart swells with excitement.

All over the hill, people raise their tent flaps and set up their wares. Music pipes from loudspeakers and we're still cutting through the people when we hear the *Toot! Toot!* coming from the Children's Train. There's a ripple of applause and laughter and it's like we're all one big family getting ready for something fantastic to happen.

I can't wait.

53

Chase

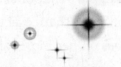

When Allie Jo showed me the phone message from Sophie's parents, I felt like stripping off my bow tie, which Dad had carefully done for me, sliding out of the vest, and heading back upstairs. I almost said so, too, but one look at Allie Jo and I knew she was counting on me. Besides, we still have to decide what to do about Tara.

As we jostle down the hall to the shuttle bus, Clay hooks up with us and starts talking to Tara. Good luck, dude.

I lean over to Allie Jo. "There's something's wrong with the way her uncle acts. Why doesn't he talk to your dad instead of bothering you?"

She glances at me real quick and talks out of the side of her mouth. "Because he knows I've seen her."

"So?" I say. "If he thinks you know something, why

doesn't he call the police? He said they were involved—right?—but I haven't seen any."

"He doesn't want to scare her," Allie Jo says. She has an answer for everything.

"When people lose their dogs, they put up signs, they tack up pictures, put notices in the newspaper." I try to think of what else they do. "They offer rewards."

Allie Jo stops walking. "That's exactly what I'm talking about." One hand goes on her hip. People flow around us. "What do you think she'd do if she saw a sign on a telephone pole with her picture on it?"

"She'd run—"

"Exactly."

"Wait. I mean she'd run because she'd know it wasn't safe to stay." And right then an idea pops in my head. "Maybe she's inherited millions of dollars and this creep of an uncle is after her so he can control the money." I rub my chin. "It makes perfect sense."

We lag behind the others. She shakes her head. "No, it doesn't. He'd be glad she was gone. He could pretend she was dead and have the money all to himself."

"Maybe that's his plan! That's why he doesn't want the police involved! He doesn't want anyone to know she's alive—that's why he kidnapped her before."

Allie Jo walks faster. I have to quicken my pace to keep up with her.

Just as we join the others, Tara turns around from up ahead as Clay heads back to the front desk.

Allie Jo says, "Or maybe he's just her uncle come to take care of her."

☾

The bus lumbers over brick roads, rocking me gently. I zonk out. After what seems like only a minute, Allie Jo jabs her elbow into my side.

"You were snoring!" She and Tara laugh. "Get up!" Allie Jo exclaims. "We're here."

We spill out of the bus and join hordes of people streaming up the hill. I've noticed that even when you don't live in a place, you find yourself scanning faces as if you'd see your friends. I don't know anyone, of course, but Allie Jo's like a celebrity making her way through the crowd. *Hello, So-and-So. Hey, there! How're you doing?* Now, if she could only get that queen wave down, she'd be set.

Dad will be here later, interviewing people and taking pictures.

I sidle up to Tara. She's very quiet and a little stiff. "You okay? You seem a little tense." Then I think how we're walking by all these *tents*—oh, man, way too much time with Allie Jo.

Tara lowers her voice. "There are many people here.

I can't track all of them, and the heat messes up their wakes." She rakes her fingers through her hair.

"Their wakes?"

"The trails they leave behind." Her eyes flit over the crowd, then back to me. "In the sea—"

Something inside me clicks into place.

"What's all this whispering?" Allie Jo crashes into the middle of us, looping one small arm around each of our backs.

I shake myself out of it. "We're feeling kinda *tents*," I say.

Allie Jo nods. "Don't be tense. You've just gotta—" Then she lifts her chin and smiles. "Oh! Good one, Chase."

Yeah, I still got it.

Chef sets us each up with a platter on which he's put fancy, miniature paper plates with one-pancake servings. Because of my cast, I hold my platter on the palm of my left hand, and I feel like a butler. *Pancake, Madam? Sir?* They go like hotcakes. Oh, too much. I crack myself up.

Allie Jo sticks to Tara, and I keep an eye on her too. I had become still when she talked about the sea. It seemed so real, so true; I felt it in my bones.

I've been over this a hundred times since last night and I still haven't figured it out. One thing is sure, though: her name isn't Pamela. I've thrown it out there a few times and she never once reacted; I don't think she'd be able to control her reflexes *that* well. My head snaps when people say *cheese*, and I've probably heard a million *cheeses* today with all the picture snapping.

Her uncle's definitely lying about her name.

Mr. Jackson gives us a break before lunch. I've passed out so many blueberry pancakes that I need to get away from that sweet smell before I barf.

"Let's go to Books 'n' Such," Allie Jo says. "I want to put my name in for a free book."

Tara watches as Chef opens the refrigerated trailer. He's getting ready to turn over for lunch, the big item being shrimp cocktail. "I'll stay here," Tara says.

Chef grins. "She's my best shrimp taster."

Tara smiles. I can tell she feels comfortable in the bubble of our tent. Allie Jo and I push our way through the surge of people. It's as crowded as a skating rink, where you have to wait for an open space to come by and jump into the flow.

We swim upstream toward the book booth, but before we get there, I pull her over to the side of a tent.

"We gotta talk about Tara," I say.

Allie Jo frowns. "I know—we have to find her uncle."

"What?" I say. "No!" Then I remind her how he's lying about her name. "He's lying about something else too."

"Like what?"

"I don't know. I just get a bad feeling from him."

Allie Jo shakes her head. "He's her uncle, and if she's

sick, she needs him. She needs to be with family." She casts her head down. "I know she said she was Selkie, but maybe that's something she needs to believe since her parents died."

"Well, my mom's gone and I haven't turned into Bigfoot."

She looks up at me. "But your mom didn't die; she just left. That's a big difference."

Fire ignites in my heart. "Yeah, that's right. Who cares when your mom just leaves." I sneer. "It makes every holiday easier, one less present to buy. No sappy Mother's Day stuff to do." I twist my head and get in her face. "Maybe *your* mom should leave and find *my* mom and they could make a club." I laugh scornfully. "What should they call it? You got any good jokes for that?"

Her big, green eyes become pools of water. "Why are you being so mean?"

"Because you act like it's no big deal my mom left." I feel my teeth showing as I talk.

"It *is* a big deal," she says, one tear slipping down her cheek. "That's why we have to find Tara's uncle."

I press my lips together. I see her tears, but I've got a bigger point to push. "Don't you see? Her uncle's lying about something."

She shakes her head. "She needs him."

"He looked kind of seedy to me, like a guy with no money."

Allie Jo looks at me with slit eyes. "What difference does it make if a person's poor? That doesn't mean they're hotel rats." Her tears evaporate. "That doesn't mean they're *seedy.*"

"Yeah, but—"

"But nothing." She wipes her eyes and says, "I'm going to the book booth." Folding herself into the crush of people, she disappears without a backward glance.

I jut my chin out. If she'd let me finish my sentence, I would've reminded her of what Tara said about the guy trying to make money off her, and how she cried when she talked about him. Even if she *is* living in a fantasy world, something's not right—something besides her head, I mean.

If I see that guy, I'm gonna ask him a bunch of questions. My brain cells explode with them on the spot, thanks to having a reporter for a dad: *What's her real name? Why are you looking for her? Where are you from?*

It occurs to me that *Smith* is a very common name. He might as well have called himself John Doe. A new question forms in my mind: *Who are you, Mr. Smith? Who are you really?*

54

Allie Jo

I can't believe Chase would make fun of someone just because they don't have money. And here's another thing—his mom's not around and that's why he doesn't understand about family, but I've got mine, and I know how important it is. That's why I'm going to see to it that Tara gets hers back.

All day long, he keeps trying to talk to me about it, and I keep shaking him off. But we're having fun too; even Tara's having fun. What with the fudge we got and the cotton candy and the magnets, spinners, and postcards, I think it's been a pretty good day.

The darkness changes everything. The sun is an orange orb melting into swirls of purple and blue. The tents glow, lit from the inside. Kids run around wearing glow-in-the-dark necklaces.

Chef's turned over for dinner, and we're now serving prime rib, small cups of Caesar salad, and Italian ice, lemon, cherry, and blueberry. I'm sampling the blueberry when I hear some girl shriek Chase's name.

A blond head bobs up and down and bursts out of the crowd. Oh, brother. It's Jennifer Jorgensen. And—oh my gosh—she's cut her hair short like Tara's. Oh. My. Gosh.

I slip the spoon out of my mouth and stare at her. She holds a big cone of cotton candy and waves it around like a scepter. The music and the sounds from the carnival games blast through the air, so I can't hear what she's saying to Chase, but from the way she keeps smiling and gesturing, I think it's safe to say she's spazzing out over him.

Tara nudges me. "Go talk to her."

No way. "I don't want to talk to her."

"Don't avoid what scares you," she says, cutting me right through to the truth.

I turn to her and look up. "She always ignores me or acts like I'm stupid. I don't want to be friends with her."

"You don't have to be friends with her," Tara says. "Just don't be scared of her." She glances their way. "I need to refill my platter," she says, then looks at mine. "So do you."

Just like that, she strides over and Jennifer and her friends make room for her. Jennifer says something, probably hello, and Tara returns the greeting. Tara comes back with a full platter and stares at me meaningfully.

"Okay, okay," I say. I put my Italian ice on her platter, then walk the same path she did, but Jennifer doesn't move for me.

"Um, excuse me," I mumble.

"Oh," she says, casting her eyes on me the same way you'd look at your shoe if you stepped in dog poop.

That just makes me mad. I glance backward at Tara, who looks at me encouragingly.

Here goes nothing. "I see you got your hair cut," I say.

She shakes her hair out. "Thank you," she says, but I don't remember giving a compliment.

"I love Tara's hair, don't you?" I ask.

"Totally." She leans out to smile at Tara.

"Thank you," I say, watching as her face draws into confusion. "I cut it."

Her lips part and her eyes widen.

Well! I've never seen her speechless. I wait for a second, then turn to Chase and say, "We better get back to work."

And with that, I pass on through and ask Chef to load my platter.

I lean against the table as I wait on him. I cannot believe what I've just done. Sneaking a glance over my shoulder, I see Jennifer and them leave. Whew. Wait till Melanie hears about this! One small step for girl; one giant leap for girlkind.

"You need to refill your platter," I say to Chase on my way back.

"Yes, ma'am," he says, snapping his heels.

I take my position next to Tara.

"Good job," she says. "Remember, you don't have to be friends, and you don't have to be enemies. Just don't be scared of her, that's the main thing."

I smile at her, then feel my heart sink. I've never had a big sister to give me advice, and other girls know a lot more than moms do. Plus, she's not afraid of anyone or anything, and she's so exciting, like how she goes swimming at night and all her stories about Selkies.

I'm going to miss her, but people belong with their family. If I were lost, I'd want someone to return me. I peer more closely through the crowd. Maybe her uncle is here.

55

Chase

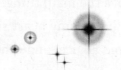

When Allie Jo trots off to use the bathroom, I sneak one of her pieces of fudge. I don't think she'll notice.

A couple stops by and takes samples off my platter. I think this is the third or fourth time they've been here, but I don't say anything. I've eaten so many samples, my gut's about to blow.

At night, the hill has a different look. Everything's in silhouette—black shapes against the darkening sky. Oak branches stretch over us like crooked fingers pointing across the crowd. I wonder if Dad's getting any good photos of this kind of stuff. I see a perfect spot looking up through the trees to the moon.

Tara walks over to me from her side and says, "Allie Jo's taking a long time."

"There's probably a line." Portable toilets in the dark. I look back at the trees; sometimes it pays to be a boy.

Mrs. Jackson left a while ago, offering to take us home as well. With two of the waitresses having just arrived, we weren't really needed anymore. But neither Allie Jo nor I wanted to leave.

I set my platter down and go through my bag of swag, as Mr. Jackson called it. The three of us had walked around earlier; pretty good take, I'd say. Bookmarks, taffy, pens with 3-D pictures on them, tokens for drinks at different restaurants—all free. I put a glowstick around my neck and crack it on.

I turn to Tara. "What are you going to do?" I ask.

She tilts her head. "What do you mean?"

I've spoken in midthought. "After tonight, what are you going to do? Are you sure you don't have someone in your family to go to, like an uncle or someone?"

She looks hurt. "My family is in the sea. Do you not believe me?"

I stare at her, then say, "I want to." At that moment, a great yearning takes over my heart, and I realize more than anything I want to believe her. I want it to be true. I want to think that magical, fantastical things are possible in this world.

"Does Allie Jo believe me?"

I chuff and raise my eyebrows. "I don't know. We've been kind of arguing on and off all day."

"About what?"

"I wish I could say." I add a shrug to make it more real, but what's really going through my mind is, *She thinks you're crazy. She wants to find your uncle.*

Oh, no. I suddenly realize where Allie Jo is.

56

Allie Jo

I've circled the tents almost three times now and tapped on the shoulders of two men who turned out not to be Tara's uncle. The crowd jostles me forward, and I stumble along. Just as I'm about to give up and head back, I spot a man near the beer tent. My heart starts up. He's got the same pear-shaped body and wiry hair.

Using my arm to split through people, I make my way over and step in front of him. It's beer he's drinking in a clear plastic cup, and by the looks of him, I doubt it's his first.

He casts a liquidy gaze on me.

"Hi," I say. "I'm Allie Jo, remember? From The Meriwether?"

His jaw moves crookedly, but he doesn't say anything.

"You were asking about Tara"—I shake my head—"I mean, Pamela."

His eyes sharpen, like shark eyes. He grabs my arm with such speed that his beer splashes on his shirt. "You know where she is, don't you?"

His sour breath splatters onto my face. Fear races up my arm and into my stomach.

"I . . . I . . . she's at our tent. You're her uncle, right?"

He laughs and pushes me away. Without waiting, he staggers through the crowd, through the big field of people, and makes a crooked path for The Meriwether tent—and Tara.

I dart through, dodging people and elbows. "Mr. Smith? Mr. Smith?" I shout. He doesn't look back. I catch up beside him. "You're her uncle, right? You're going to help her."

Some teenage boys bluster by, bumping into me and knocking me backward. They don't even stop to see if I'm okay. I pick myself up and jump up and down to spot him.

I see the top of his head as he makes wobbly progress toward The Meriwether tent, and suddenly I realize what I've done. I charge through people, tripping over their feet, pushing some of them out of the way.

"Tara!" I start yelling. "Tara!"

57

Chase

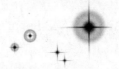

Fireworks scream through the air, then *BOOM! BOOM! BOOM!* Red, white, and blue stars explode in the sky.

"Whoo!" I shout along with the crowd. The stars whistle, leaving trails of color as they fall to the ground.

BOOMBOOM! White flash pots blast so loudly, my heart feels them.

"Yeah!" I pump my fist and glance toward Tara.

She's crouched at the foot of the table, eyes skyward and full of fear. Her platter and samples lie scattered in the grass.

I shout in her direction. "It's just—" She can't hear me over the crowd and fireworks. I slide my platter on Chef's table, walk over, and crouch beside Tara.

"It's just fireworks!" Even this close, I yell to be heard.

She looks at me, but she doesn't seem to recognize my

words. Her eyes are huge—coal black circles. Without saying anything, she grasps me by the cast.

Pop. KABOOM! Golden sparkles sizzle in the sky.

Gesturing upward with my good arm, I lean toward her ear. "It's just for fun," I shout. But in this closeness, in this dark nearness, I suddenly feel terror. Her hand slips into mine.

BANG! Whiz! BANG! BANG! Purple, green, purple.

"Tara!"

I'm sure I heard someone call Tara's name. The crowd in the middle is still, but in front of the booths, people mix and mill about, merging like traffic. I pull Tara to her feet.

KAPOW!

"Tara!"

We both hear that. I scan the crowd and spot Allie Jo. I start to laugh when I see her bumping through the crowd, leaving a trail of annoyed people behind her.

But then I see her face.

Her features are strained, her voice ragged. "Run, Tara, run!" she yells.

Tara's uncle emerges from the mob. His beady eyes lock onto Tara and he moves like a steamroller, plowing people down as he makes his way toward us.

"Come on!" I yank Tara hard and start running.

58

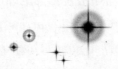

It was him.

Her heart exploded into a million pieces, splintering like the colors in the sky.

BOOM! BOOM!

"Come on!" Chase yelled, yanking her away from the tent.

She snapped at Chase's command. Tearing through the crowd, she glided easily through people wading up the hill. Power coursed through her veins, making her legs faster, almost giving her flight. At the bottom of the hill, she leaped off the curb.

An angry horn blared. Tires screeched, but she kept running.

The horrible sound of the sky splitting cracked overhead. She didn't want to stay in this confusing world, with its harsh noise and strange ways. She looked back to see Chase close behind, followed by Allie Jo, and blundering down the hill was the man.

Allie Jo pointed between buildings. "This way!"

Tara and Chase turned back quickly and caught up to her.

Allie Jo led them through narrow passageways between crumbling buildings. They jumped over a low fence; Tara heard it crack behind her as the man tried to hurdle it.

Rounding a corner, they hopped another fence and shot into the woods. Tara's heart beat hard and strong. She controlled her breathing, for she didn't know how long they would run. As they dashed by old oaks and tall maples, Tara began to hear the whispers. They were near The Meriwether.

The three raced in silence, save for the branches and twigs that snapped as they passed. Tara heard the man beating his way through the trees. The cruel sound of his breathing reached her ears.

When they cleared the wood line, they ran in plain sight across the mowed lawn of the hotel.

The man laughed sneeringly from the trees.

59

Allie Jo

"Come on, come on," I urge hoarsely, pressing open the panel to the secret nanny staircase.

Chase starts pounding up the stairs. The wood screams his every step.

"NO!" I swing the door shut. "He'll hear you."

"But—" Chase cuts himself off as we hear the door to the sunporch blast open. Heavy footsteps stumble into the hotel.

In the darkness of the staircase, I hold my breath.

Each footfall is a threat. His ragged gasping is a curse in my ears. If only the hotel could swallow him up and flush him out, but, no, it can't—I'm the one who brought him here.

I betrayed her.

I'm horrible. I'm no good. I'm the worst person in the world.

His footsteps plod past us. Chase stirs, but Tara whispers, "Be still."

If she'll stay here after this, I promise to never tell anyone about her. Just let her forgive me.

Before I can think another thought, her hand grasps mine and holds it tightly.

We're about to move when we hear Clay's voice coming down the hallway. "You say they went up through the panel?"

"Run!" I shout.

60

Chase

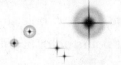

We pound up the stairs, not caring about the noise. Light gleams in as Clay opens the door. "Allie Jo?" he calls.

I lean over the banister and see Mr. Smith craning his neck to spot us. Without even thinking, I grab the old window hook from the landing and hurl it down. My left arm's a bad shot, but it comes close enough to buy us a few seconds.

"Fifth floor!" I shout, hoping to mislead him. I burst out onto the fourth floor.

Tara and Allie Jo tear through behind me. My eyes quickly adjust to the darkness. Allie Jo bends down to catch her breath. Through a broken window, I hear a faint sizzle, then red shards explode in the sky.

Muffled footsteps creak from the secret staircase.

"Look at the elevator!" Allie Jo says. The elevator light

flashes numbers: 2 . . . 3 . . . They have to get out at four; the elevator doesn't go up to the nanny quarters.

Footsteps, the elevator's ancient rattle, and the thunder of fireworks in the sky.

They're closing in on us.

Shoving open the door to the service stairs, I yell, "Come on!"

Just as Tara and Allie Jo bolt through, the elevator doors part and light pours onto its only passenger.

Mr. Smith.

61

Allie Jo

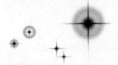

We race down the stairs into the tunnels.

Darkness flows around us, but I know this place like the back of my hand. I swing open the cedar-planked door on the right. Tara slips right in. Chase moves with his hand on the wall. I grab him, shut the door swiftly behind us, and lower the bar. We're in the speakeasy. I check the porthole—closed.

"Shh," I say, putting my fingers to my lips. We pad to the farthest wall and slip down to the floor, each of us breathing heavily as quietly as we can.

Footsteps echo in the tunnel.

My whole body becomes an antenna, alert to every sound and movement.

He attacks the brick walls in a burst of pounding. "I know you're here!" he rasps. "Come on out, seal girl." His voice goes in a direction opposite of us. I hear his feet shuffle off toward the entrance. "I've got something for you."

Tara stiffens.

"It's a trick," I whisper softly. "Don't listen to him."

"My skin." The words slip out of her mouth.

Before I can stop her, she leaps to the door.

62

Chase

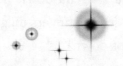

I spring up and snatch Tara back from the door. "Don't!"

Lit by the green glowstick still around my neck, her face takes on an ethereal quality, as if the color of the springs was being reflected on her cheeks. She is full of moonbeams.

Allie Jo rushes up to her and shakes her head. "Stay here."

Tara's eyes glow from behind.

All of a sudden, her uncle lets loose with a barrage of pounding. The thick door shakes. Then he whams the door with something heavy. The wood cracks, splinters.

I throw the bar off, time my move, and smash the door into him.

"Run!" I shout, sprinting up the service stairs. Tara's

even faster. As we get to the first-floor landing, I turn the knob, but the door's locked. I beat it with my fists.

"Clay!" I shout. I know he's got to be close by. "Clay!"

Allie Jo screams.

I turn around and see he's got Allie Jo by the arm on the lower landing. She tries to wrench out of his grip, but he's too strong. Tears streak down her face. In the dim light of the stairs, I see his fingers digging into her flesh.

I take a few steps down.

"Don't do it." His voice comes out low and menacing.

"Let her go," Tara says.

"It's been a long trip lookin' for you," he says to her, not distracted by Allie Jo's struggling. "I'm not leaving without you." Then he looks at Allie Jo and gestures his head at her. "Or maybe I'll take her."

I look around for something to throw at him. There's only one thing.

I spring from the steps like I'm doing an ollie. Snapping up my legs, I crash into him and we fall backward. My cast cracks against the floor, sending a surge of pain up my arm.

He stands and when I clamber to get up, he slams me down. I collapse in a heap by his feet. My vision blurs. I'm stunned, like when I hit my head falling off the skateboard.

"Leave him alone," Tara says.

I try to focus, but there's two of her. They move closer.

"That's right, girlie," he sneers. "You come with me."

"No." The Taras set their faces. They look like Amazons, with their short, blond hair.

"Oh, I think you will." From under his shirt, he pulls out some kind of wadding.

It grazes me as he holds it up. It's nice and furry, soft. I want to pull it around myself.

The Taras gasp. "My skin!"

My head floats in circles. I squint to turn her back into one person.

She grits her teeth. All that stands between her and the water is her skin.

I summon up all my energy and smash his knees with my cast. He crumples to the ground. I snatch up the skin.

"The springs!" I yell.

63

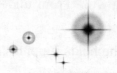

As they flew across the lawn, Chase tossed the skin to her. She stretched her arms toward it, drawing it in close after catching it.

Her skin! Her legs took her swiftly even as she cried out in joy, caressing the skin. Tears, human tears, rolled down her face; a wave of longing surged in her soul. Green and blue images of the salty depths flooded her spirit and she trilled loudly, bidding her distant cousins to come to her aid. They knew these waters and could show her the way to the seas.

In the darkness at the water's edge, she ripped off the human clothing, foreign to her even in their skin, and slipped her own luxurious sealskin over her feet and onto her shoulders.

Allie Jo stumbled forward, crying. "I'm sorry," she said. "I thought he was your uncle and I wanted to help you. I—"

Tara held Allie Jo's face in both her hands. "You are good," she said, and kissed her lightly on the cheek.

Chase loped over, stopped in front of her. Tumbling currents of confusion rolled off him, but they did not obscure his heart from her.

Tara grabbed him fiercely. "Thank you," she said. Wetness touched her cheek as she hugged him, and she realized tears flowed from his eyes as well.

"Hey!" The sweaty blobfish man hobbled from the tunnel, followed by Clay, who jogged after him, yelling into his walkie-talkie.

Tara's face hardened as she looked at the man and remembered his plans for her. She squeezed Chase one more time and kissed him on the cheek.

Overwhelmed with joy, she flashed them a big smile and dove into the water.

64

Allie Jo

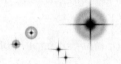

Clay takes one look at me and tackles Mr. Smith, or whoever he really is. Minutes later, the police arrive and get our stories. Chase and I tell them everything—how that man grabbed me, how he said he was going to take me, how he slapped Chase down—we tell them everything except about Tara.

The officers lead him away in handcuffs. The whole way to the patrol car, he's spouting off about a seal girl and a skin. We shake our heads like he's crazy.

My arm's purpling up really badly, and Chase is acting woozy.

"Know what?" he says to Clay. "I think I've got a concussion."

"Don't worry," Clay says. He gestures toward the police. "They called for an ambulance. Can you make it back in?"

Chase gives him a lopsided smile. "Totally, dude."

Clay cracks a grin. "Okay, *dude*." He makes us sit in the office, "where I can keep an eye on you," he says.

Through the window, I see the police waiting for the ambulance to arrive. Moments later, our parents rush in, looking all worried and scared. The room bursts with voices and movement, and Chase and I tell once again about the crazy man harassing us, thinking we had something that belonged to him.

When the ambulance comes, Chase raises two fingers. "Peace out," he says to me.

"See ya later, alligator," I respond.

☾

In the snuggly blankets of my bed, I can't fall asleep. It's not my arm, which is really sore, and I'm not scared, like if that man could escape.

It's just I can't stop thinking about Tara.

"You are good," she'd said and kissed me. Then she hugged Chase too.

My eyes got blurry with tears after she dove into the springs, but I know I saw what I saw: a seal bobbed up and winked at me.

65

Chase

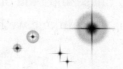

The doctor at the hospital diagnosed me with a mild concussion and, after taking X-rays, said my arm was fine and healing in the right places. A week later, my headaches are gone and my arm is fine.

Allie Jo and I decided it was best to keep Tara's story to ourselves; we couldn't risk more Mr. Smiths looking to make money off Selkies. We didn't even tell Sophie, and we saw her nearly every day. Sophie and Allie Jo have been knitting furiously, as if they have some kind of deadline. Which I guess they do. Sophie and her family are leaving today.

I get up quickly and slap the button on the alarm. Let Dad sleep; he deserves it. I pull on my shorts and a blue skateboard shirt, brush my teeth, and try to fix my hair, which is standing up at all angles. Rub in a little of Dad's gel and, yeah, my hair's chillin'.

Before I leave the room, I grab the little white box that's been sitting for weeks on my nightstand and slip it into one of my pockets. It's now or never.

Mrs. Duran, Sophie, and Allie Jo are sitting in the parlor by the grand staircase when I come down. Mr. Duran's getting the suitcases together and finalizing his bill with Mr. Jackson.

"Morning," I say, acting all casual even though my heart beats a million miles a minute. They all look up at me, smile, murmur, "Good morning," and "Hi, Chase," and I realize I need to get Sophie alone if I'm going to do this.

I look right at her. "One last game of air hockey?" I ask.

Allie Jo stands up. "Sounds good to me. Sophie can be on your team on account of your arm."

No, no, no! I shout in my mind. But what can I do with Mrs. Duran sitting right there? When we turn down the hall, my hand slips into Sophie's and she squeezes back, causing my heart to overflow. I wonder if this is what love feels like.

"Allie Jo, could you go back?" I blurt.

She furrows her eyebrows for a second, then glances at our hands and smiles. "Oh. *Lovebird* stuff."

My face heats up. Sophie giggles.

After we're alone, I take Sophie into the game room and tell her I don't want to play games. "I have something to say."

Her blue eyes sparkle up at me. It's a rush having her look at me this way.

My lips open and close. I gaze into her eyes and that calms me. "I like you," I say.

She breaks out in a big smile. "I like you too."

My heart soars. I dig into my pocket and open the box.

Her hands fly in front of her face. "Oh! It's so pretty!"

"A green heart," I say. "Just like the one you gave me." I gesture with my cast.

Then I take the ring and slip it onto the third finger of her right hand. "If I could, I would put it on your other hand."

She turns her face up to mine, and I kiss her softly, hug her tightly.

Then she's gone.

☾

Later, I grab my skateboard and head up to the third floor, laughing at the *Guests Prohibited* sign. Ah, the third floor; so nice, so long. So perfect.

I slap the board down and plant my right foot near the

tail. Pushing off with my left, I glide down the hallway, stopping at the place I fell before. I pop the board up.

"Hey!"

I whip my head around and see a girl standing all sergeantlike, hands on her hips, legs apart. I grin, throw my board down, and I'm off.

She pounds down the hallway. "Is it time for my lesson yet?" she shouts.

I laugh. "Come and get me!"

66

Allie Jo

"I got this for you," Nicholas says to Chase. From his pocket, he hands him a little red car. "I got it at a party, but I don't like it, so I'm giving it to you for going away."

Chase examines it properly in his hand, shoves it into his pocket, and pats Nicholas on the head. "Thanks, bud. I'll take good care of it."

We stand in the front-desk area on one of the worst days of summer. Chase is leaving today. But I remind myself that Melanie will be back in ten days.

Ryan gives Chase a quarter and a drawing of a stickman that's supposed to be Chase. The head is fifty times larger than the body, and the stick arm has a circle on it.

I bend down to Ryan's height, making sure my newly

finished scarf doesn't drag on the floor. "Good job, Ryan. Is that Chase's cast?"

He nods, looks shyly up to Chase, who makes a big show of inspecting the picture.

"I'm definitely framing this when I get home," Chase says.

Ryan's cheeks puff out with a great big smile.

"You boys run back to your room now," I say. "Your mom's waiting on you."

Mr. Dennison trudges over from the front desk with Clay, carrying suitcases and his typewriter. Chase and I trail behind them, past the grand staircase, past the game room, out to the parking lot and their car.

As they load up, I say to Chase, "I'll never forget this summer."

"Me neither," he says. "I'll never tell either."

I nod my agreement. We sigh, looking at each other. The sun beats down, promising to fry the skin right off my bones this afternoon. I hand him an envelope with my address and a stamp already on it. "Make sure you write me."

"I will." Neither of us smiles.

Clay claps Chase on the back. "Be cool."

Chase grins. "I'm always cool, dude!"

"Oh, Allie Jo," Mr. Dennison says. He shakes Clay's

hand before Clay leaves; then he comes over to me with a big envelope. "I had some extra photos made for you." He slides one out.

The deep emerald green water of Hope Springs shimmers in waves, and the plants and pebbles below look purple. I see big shapes in the shadows.

"Manatees!" I say.

"Sea cows," Mr. Dennison replies.

Chase and I laugh. "They hate that name," we say at the same time.

I give Chase a bear hug before he climbs into the car. A world of understanding passes between us.

Their car crunches over the gravel, then spins out some dirt as Mr. Dennison turns onto the driveway.

My mouth quivers, but I wave my arm wildly. "Bye, Chase!"

Chase sticks his head out the window. "Bye, Allie Jo!" he yells. Mr. Dennison toots the horn a few times.

I sit on the porch steps and watch Chase waving his cast at me all the way down the driveway until I can't see them anymore. Even then I stare after him for a minute.

The morning breeze ruffles my hair and whispers through the trees. A couple of lizards dart by my feet. Lizard earrings. I can't wait till Melanie gets back. I've got so much to tell her and a lot I can't tell her, but at least I can teach her to knit. I glance over to the jacaranda, standing in a pool of its own lavender petals, and I see Jinx up high, crossing the branch to our garden room.

I guess that's enough sitting on my butt for one morning. I whirl my scarf around my neck and stand up. Time to get started on my rounds.

ACKNOWLEDGMENTS

I'm grateful to many people for helping me bring *The Summer of Moonlight Secrets* to life. First off, thanks to God for letting me write stories for a living; my agent, Ted Malawer, for his advice and encouragement; Joe Alvarado, Jerilyn Meagher, and Billy Meagher for sharing their broken-arm experiences with me; Steve Haworth for describing his snorkeling adventures to me; and special thanks to Alessandra Josephine Furnari for allowing me to use her nickname, Allie Jo.

My family supports and believes in me: Zachary, Matthew, Brooke, Steve, Michelle, Mike, and Mom—I love you!

Emily Easton of Walker Books made a suggestion that broke the story open for me, and Brandon Dorman created a cover illustration that is absolutely beautiful and conveys the pure essence of the book.

Finally, I want to thank Stacy Cantor, my editor at Walker Books. Stacy possesses an uncanny knack for teasing out all the best parts of a story, and I consider it a blessing to work with such a talented editor.

Joshua Reed is used to being the new kid. But he never expected to find a friend like Jack . . .

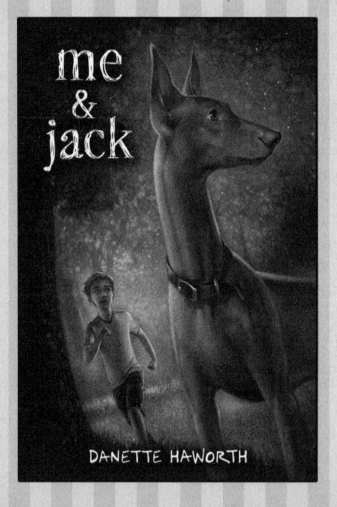

Read on for a sneak peek at this exciting adventure!

We ducked into the garage and I rolled out my bike. The hill we lived on was so steep I had to brake all the way down. Jack jogged easily at my side; he didn't seem to mind the leash at all. At the bottom of the hill, we turned right. I picked up speed and Jack ran faster, too. He looked like a racehorse. I pedaled as fast as I could, and he matched me.

We coasted around the bend, and I saw a couple of boys playing basketball in a driveway. I took a deep breath and slowed down as we got closer to them. My first new people. Having done this a million times, I knew how to make my approach—say hi; don't act too eager; play it cool—but I still always got that nervous feeling in the pit of my stomach. One kid had wavy, light blond hair, and he dribbled the ball toward me. The other kid was average in every way—not fat, not skinny, a little taller than me but not like a giant or anything. He acted like I wasn't there. I did notice he had kind of a big butt.

"Hi," the blond kid said.

I gave him the head jerk, that quick kind of nod that means hello. I don't like to act too friendly at first, because you can't take any of it back if the other kid doesn't like you. Still, he did walk over to me and that was a good sign. I squeezed my brakes and put my foot down. Jack stopped, too, standing at attention by my side. The mailbox read "Miller."

The blond kid dribbled the ball in place a few times, then said, "I like your dog."

"Thanks. His name's Jack," I said. Jack huffed a little when he heard his name. "I got him at the pound."

The other kid shifted on his feet. "Come on, Ray." He wiped his forehead with his arm. I saw he wore a leather wristband. Pretty cool. But he didn't even glance at me, so I didn't say anything to him.

Ray knelt down to pet Jack, but Jack backed away from him. "It's okay, boy," Ray said, holding out his hand for Jack to smell. Jack backed against my leg and looked at me.

"He just has to get used to things," I said. I leaned over and petted Jack so he wouldn't feel all alone.

The screen door wrenched open. A little girl leaned out and yelled, "Alan, Mom's coming—oh! *Doggie!*"

New kid rule: always listen. The other kid's name was

Alan, and he must be the little girl's brother. I filed that information in my head.

She skipped down the porch and right up to Jack. Jack didn't even move away.

"Wow," I said.

Still squatting, Ray said, "He likes you, CeeCee."

It was true. Jack nudged his head into her hand, the better for petting.

"I like him, too," CeeCee said. She tipped her face up to me. "Are you his dog?"

"No," I said, feeling the corner of my mouth lift into a grin. "I'm his human."

Alan clucked his tongue. "Get away from him, CeeCee!"

I couldn't tell if he was talking about me or Jack.

CeeCee acted as if she hadn't heard him. "Hi, doggie!" She patted his head and scratched his ears.

"I said get *away* from that dog!" Alan said. "Plus, I thought you said Mom was coming."

CeeCee stood and twisted her face at him. "You're not the boss of me."

"It's okay, Alan," Ray said and stood up. "This dog's okay." Then to me, "Is he a show dog?"

Before I could answer, Alan sighed loudly and dragged himself closer, but he stopped short of joining us. "Why does he have red around his eyes?" he asked, curling up the corner of his mouth. "Is he sick or something? He looks weird."

My eyes narrowed. "He's not weird."

He raised his chin at me. "Well, he looks weird. What kind of dog is he?"

"A good dog," I said, gripping my handlebars tightly.

The kid sneered, then shouted, "His nose is turning pink! Oh man! What a weird dog—you should've named him Rudolph." He shook his head. "Wonder why the pound didn't kill him." Then he snatched the ball from Ray and ran down the driveway. "C'mon, Ray!" He shot the ball through the hoop. "Yeah! Two points! Later, kid!"

I wanted to shout—I don't know what I wanted to shout—but my mouth and my brain got stuck.

"Come on, CeeCee!" he yelled. "That dog might bite you."

CeeCee stared at her brother with her lip stuck out. Then she turned to me, her eyes big and blue. In a soft little voice, she asked, "He won't bite me . . . right?"

I bent down to face her. "Of course not! He's a nice dog. Plus, he likes you."

She looked up at me and smiled. "What's your name?"

"Joshua."

"I'm CeeCee."

Ray stood. "I'm Ray. Your dog's cool."

"Thanks." I tried to look friendly, but I had a hard time concentrating on it. "Who's that kid?"

"Do you know Prater Lumber?" Ray asked. When I shook my head, he said, "Well, he's Alan Prater." Ray made it sound important; I added a mental note to my file.

I watched as Ray pulled a yo-yo from his pocket, throwing it down hard, then flicking it up to wind the string around his fingers in a web. It should have knotted, but then he slapped his hand and the yo-yo spun down and back up into his hand.

"Nice." I'd only seen that kind of stuff on TV.

Ray grinned and spun the yo-yo absentmindedly while he talked. "I'm working on a combo for the July Fourth festival. Hopefully, I'll have enough saved up for the Groove-it by then."

"What's that?"

He caught the yo-yo around his back. "It's a better yo-yo for string tricks."

Closer to the garage, Alan bounced the basketball from side to side. "Ray! Put the stupid yo-yo down and let's play already."

An expression passed over Ray's face so quickly, I almost missed it—he pressed his lips together and rolled his eyes. I glanced toward the hoop, where Alan Prater made easy baskets from the side. Probably thought he was a big shot. If I called him Alan, he'd think we were friends or something. I'd call him Prater.

Ray slipped the yo-yo into his pocket.

"So he doesn't live here?" I asked.

"He's my brother," CeeCee said. "He's twelve and I'm five. I'll be in kindergarten next year. Alan's scared of dogs." She fished in the pocket of her shorts. "Do you like candy?"

Whoa, scared of dogs. I fixed my eyes on Prater. "Yeah . . ."

"Want one?" She held out a butterscotch to me. It looked kind of grubby, and lint stuck to the parts that weren't wrapped, but I took it anyway. Every new kid knows that rule: never say no to friendliness.

She popped one into her mouth and started talking about Missy, her best friend who she saw every day, and they liked to play dolls, except Missy has the most important one, which is the Ken doll, and everyone knows the girl doll needs a boyfriend, but CeeCee doesn't have one and—

Prater's afraid of dogs. I wanted to get back to that but didn't know how.

"Come on!" Prater shouted from the hoop.

We watched as Prater threw the ball but missed. Guess he wasn't as good as he thought he was. He looked up and caught me staring. "Take a picture, why don't you?"

I would, but it would probably break the camera. That's what I wanted to say. Instead, I stood there like an idiot.

Ray asked, "You want to play?"

Yeah, but not with Prater around. Sometimes you have to break your own rules. I shook my head. I wasn't saying no to friendliness—I was saying no to Prater. "I have to take Jack for a walk."

I couldn't wait to get away from there. Jack and I rode back the same way we came. Prater the pear. Prater the crater. Prater the hater. Ray was okay, but Prater was a jerk.

DANETTE HAWORTH

is the author of *Me & Jack*, *The Summer of Moonlight Secrets*, and *Violet Raines Almost Got Struck by Lightning*. She held a number of writing jobs before turning to fiction, including positions as a technical writer and a travel writer. Danette lives in Orlando, Florida, and blogs regularly.

www.danettehaworth.com

Ready to dare?

Try one of these great reads about finding yourself and following your dreams . . .

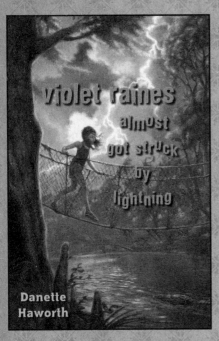

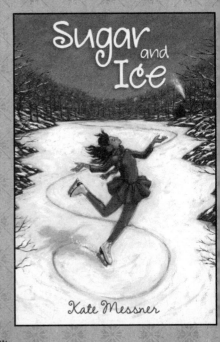

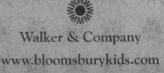